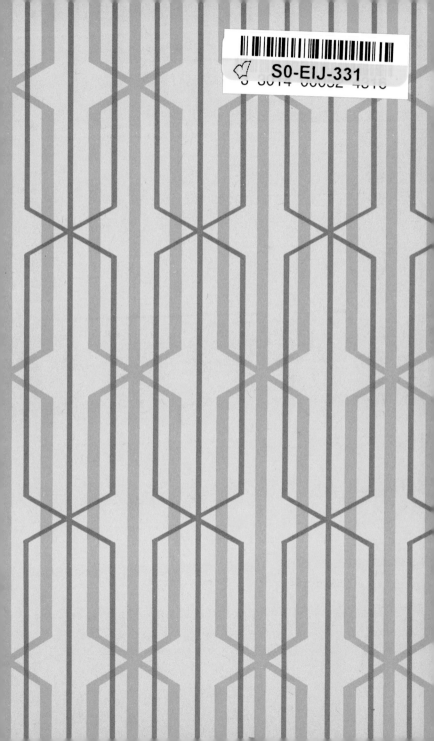

BAR 1

ROUNDUP OF BEST WESTERN STORIES

BAR 1

Roundup of Best Western Stories

Selected and With Introductions

by

SCOTT MEREDITH

Short Story Index Reprint Series

BOOKS FOR LIBRARIES PRESS
FREEPORT, NEW YORK

COPYRIGHT OF INDIVIDUAL STORIES

Posse by C. Hall Thompson appeared originally in *Esquire*. Copyright 1951 by Esquire, Inc.

Well of Anger by Morgan Lewis appeared originally in *The Saturday Evening Post*. Copyright 1950 by The Curtis Publishing Company.

Two-Faced Promise by Bill Gulick appeared originally in *Dime Western*. Copyright 1951 by Popular Publications, Inc.

The Fraudulent Skunk by A.B. Guthrie, Jr., appeared originally in *Collier's*. Copyright 1951 by the Crowell-Collier Publishing Company.

Lonesome Ride by Ernest Haycox appeared originally in *The Saturday Evening Post* under the title of *Dead-Man Trail*, and in the book, *Rough Justice*, published by Little, Brown and Company, under its present title. Copyright 1948 by The Curtis Publishing Company. Copyright 1950 by Ernest Haycox.

Pride in His Holsters by Robert W. Lowndes appeared originally in *Dime Western* under the title of *The Last Four Kings*. Copyright 1948 by Popular Publications, Inc.

A Man Called Horse by D. M. Johnson appeared originally in *Collier's*. Copyright 1951 by Dorothy M. Johnson.

The Ghost Lode by William Brandon appeared originally in *The American Magazine*. Copyright 1950 by The Crowell-Collier Publishing Company.

The Man at Gantt's Place by Steve Frazee appeared originally in *Argosy*. Copyright 1951 by Popular Publications, Inc.

Campaigning Cowpoke by Clark Gray appeared originally in *Zane Grey's Western Magazine*. Copyright 1951 by The Hawley Publications, Inc.

The Sound of Gunfire by John O'Reilly appeared originally in *Famous Western*. Copyright 1949 by Columbia Publications, Inc.

Sergeant Houck by Jack Schaefer appeared originally in *Colliers*. Copyright 1951 by Jack Schaefer.

STANDARD BOOK NUMBER:

8369-3032-0

LIBRARY OF CONGRESS CATALOG CARD NUMBER:

79-75782

MANUFACTURED
BY
HALLMARK LITHOGRAPHERS, INC.
IN THE U.S.A.

To Steve

CONTENTS

INTRODUCTION

IF THIS anthology of Western stories were being prepared and published in 1920 or 1930 rather than at the present time, the reader could be reasonably sure of finding certain familiar things in nearly every one of the selections. For example:

1. The hero of nearly every story would be an iron-nerved gentleman who was absolutely unfamiliar with the sensation of fear. Even if he were being chased by sixty-seven men armed with two guns and a knife apiece—a circumstance which would cause most men in real life to shiver right out of their trousers—the Western-story hero would just yawn and continue to lope calmly along.

2. The Indians in the stories would be unthinking savages who spent all of their time tracking down and killing white men—doing their stuff for no reason other than blood-lust and the joy of killing. You would practically never find the suggestion that sometimes Indian attacks were justified and pretty much in the nature of self-defense.

3. The Western hero might sometimes kiss his horse, but never his girl friend. (As a matter of fact, the girl in the average Western story circa 1920 usually had so little to do that considerable interested speculation has been devoted to the question of why female characters were included in the first place.) . . . At any rate, you'd certainly find that the male-female relationships in Western stories were non-romantic, non-intimate, and positively non-sexual. There were, of course, children in the stories, sometimes, but these presumably arrived in some entirely pure manner — perhaps astride storks.

4. The towns would be populated almost entirely with wandering cowhands, gamblers, lawmen, gunmen, and saloon-keepers. The less glamourous residents—the storekeepers, the feed merchants, the town doctors, the lawyers, and so on—would sometimes be mentioned in passing, but were rarely considered interesting and exciting enough to be given the stature of major characters, even though they may well have been the real backbone of the real Old West.

5. In general, the plots and characters would be enormously oversimplified—with the villain nearly always an out-and-out crook (the crooked banker out to steal the land or the crooked foreman out to steal the cattle,) and the hero all too often an out-and-out angel who had no personal stake in the matter but helped defeat the bad guys because he was a good guy. Characters would rarely be understandable human beings whom circumstances and conflicting points of view had placed on opposite sides of the fence: villains were all-black, villainous in everything they said or did or thought, and heroes were all-white, entirely pure at all times.

These things, and others like them, were practically traditional in the Western story of some years ago—always excepting the yarns by the few writers who were ahead of their time—but, after a while, intelligent and thoughtful Western readers began to rebel against them because they were so obviously synthetic. More and more readers began to complain that, even in frontier life with men well-acquainted with bloodshed and sudden death, a man is still going to get a frightened sensation in the stomach when people start pumping lead at him—many Indians were the victims of incredibly cruel and treacherous treatment by white men, and attacked wagon trains in the same way that you and I would defend our land against invaders—romantic and sexual activities formed as important a part of life in the Old West as anywhere else in the world—and a little more attention to storekeepers and farmers and other less-publicized figures of the Old West, and a little more attention to the subtleties of human behavior and human relations, might be a sensible move.

And the result of this attitude on the part of readers—the result of the dissatisfaction with the stereotyped, or cornball, variety of Western story—has been the current story of the Old West, unarguably the Western at its best in history. To-day's better Western story goes far beyond the Class G movie level, the I - jest - happened - to - be - moseyin' - along - playin' - my - guitar - Ma'am - and - I - overheered - yore - foreman - plottin' - some - rustlin' class: it portrays the Old West as it really was, and its people think and act like people.

The nice thing about it all, too, is that the current Western is even more interesting and exciting than the old-style horse opry. Perhaps it's because you can *believe* the modern West-ern yarn and its characters instead of having to keep fighting off the feeling that you're reading about a slightly ridiculous never-never land; or perhaps it's because the current Western, with its deeper probing of people and emotions, requires better writing and better writers and therefore means better stories. Whatever the reason, the fast-moving, plausible, com-pletely enjoyable current Western has brought about a ren-aissance in the field, a new upsurge of popularity—one example of which is visible in the fact that every major Hollywood studio now regularly makes Class A Westerns featuring its top stars.

This book, a sampler collection of twelve Western stories selected from the thousands published in recent years, covers nearly every locale and every type of human being within the Old West. You'll find Indian country and farming country, busy wide-open towns and the lonely desert, a young kid contemplating the owlhoot trail and an old prospector con-templating murder, a tired and cynical hired gunman and a man who never used a gun. Each of the stories is the current Western at its best.

INTRODUCTION

A number of years ago, this writer lived briefly in an old house in a New Mexico town, just a short distance from the place at which Billy the Kid was killed. One of the rooms in the house had been a rendezvous for Wild West outlaws, and a scar on the bureau-top was reputed to have been made when Billy the Kid slammed his gun-butt down in a rage.

Outside the house, sleek new cars rolled along the highway, and people walked calmly back and forth on their twentieth-century pursuits, but that room was a world unto itself; it was still genuine frontier in there. That is the way it is with the stories in this volume, and perhaps that is their chief charm: they've a feeling of authenticity about them. I hope you'll agree that the opening paragraphs of each story is a private doorway back in the colorful and rip-snortin' Old West.

Scott Meredith

POSSE

By C. HALL THOMPSON

POSSE is the story of Billy Reo, four-time killer who had seen a hanging as a kid and never forgotten its horror, and of the things that happened to him when his own time came. There's no sweetness and light in this piece: it's a grim and realistic story with an especially macabre ending.

BILLY REO was dreaming again. The pain in the small of his back where buckshot had riddled the intestines seemed far away now and he was not lying in the loft of an abandoned barn; he could not smell the hay nor hear the rats squealing in the empty stalls below.

He was back in a town in the Panhandle and he was nineteen and had never watched a man die. A mob jostled along the main square. He could see the red, mustached faces of furious men and hear them yelling, "Lynch the murdering greaser! Bust into the cell and string him up!"

Then he saw two townsmen come out through the jail door, dragging the Mexican boy between them. He heard the boy praying and moaning, and followed the mob across the dusty wide square to the big oak. The boy was crying softly and someone larruped the flank of the pony and it jolted out from under and the boy screamed only once before the hemp snapped his spine.

13

And, here in the barn loft, Reo could see the boy's face, twisted at a crazy angle by the knot under the left ear. Only now it was his own face; it was Billy Reo who danced there above the stiff white masks of the mob.

"No!"

He lurched to a sitting position.

The stab of fire along his back brought him full awake. Sweat wilted the blond bristles of his jaw. It stung his eyes. He sank back, breathing too hard.

Get hold of yourself, he thought. *Let them form their damned posse. They'll never find you here.*

They had never caught him before. In the ten years since he had drifted north into the territories, Billy Reo had killed four men. Riding from one gun town to the next, he had learned the lightning downsweep and rise of hand that could put three slugs into a man's belly before he sprawled in the dust. And the killing had been a safe, secret thing. People had looked at him and wondered, maybe, but no one had ever been able to prove his suspicions.

Safe and easy, his mind said. And this time was no different.

Only this time *was* different. This time it had been in a grubby saloon in Alamosa with a mob of witnesses right on the spot.

He hadn't figured the greenhorn to call his bluff. The greenhorn, a spindly kid named Reckonridge, had looked as if he never left mama's side. Reo and Jack Larin had idled into the bar to wash the red dust out of their tonsils and had seen this kid sporting a load of double eagles. It wasn't hard to talk up a game of deuces wild. It should have been easy to slip that deuce off the bottom when the pot was at its peak.

But Reckonridge had a quick eye and a temper to match. He had cursed and dropped one hand below the table. Reo never stopped to argue. A beer-blown blonde had screamed. The shots had sounded very loud and Reckonridge had gone over backward, still seated, with two small holes in his chest.

The saloon crowd had not moved. Elbow to elbow, guns level, Reo and Larnin had backed through swinging doors to the ponies at the hitch. They had swung up and wheeled west and, in that moment Rio had seen the long, loose-limbed man come running through the moonlight; glimpsed the lifting shotgun, the flash of a metal star against a black vest.

"Ride, Jack! Ride like hell!"

Slapping heels to the roan's flanks, he had bent low. But not low enough. He had felt the fire needles burn into his back almost before he heard the slam and echo of the double barrels. Somehow, he had kept the roan haunch to haunch with Larin's pinto. Somehow, he had ridden.

Reo was sweating again. The blood-wet flannel shirt stuck to his back. His legs had a numbness that frightened him. *Witnesses*, he thought. This time there was proof. This time, the man in the black vest would talk. The citizens of Alamosa would swear in as deputies. Before daylight, the posse would lead out. Maybe even now . . .

"Damn," he said hoarsely.

His head rolled from side to side. He could see the

Mexican boy very clearly; the hard, implacable faces of the mob, the sudden, singing wrench of the rope.

"Billy."

His body stiffened. A hand clawed for the pistol that lay by his hip. He caught the scrape of boots on the ladder; a light shaft cut up through the loft trap. Then the lean, flat-planed face and narrow shoulders came into view, one fist holding high the lantern, and Jack Larnin said, "Easy, Billy. Just me."

The gun hand relaxed.

Larnin set down the lamp. It was hooded so that only a thin yellow beam broke the darkness.

Reo's eyes narrowed. "Well?"

Larnin stood tall above him. A rat rustled in the hay. Light shimmered on the dainty needlework of a spider's web. Larnin said, "How's the wound?"

Reo looked at him. "The wound's all right. I'm not thinking about the wound."

The silent question hung between them. Reo felt sweat cold along his ribs.

Finally Larnin looked away, said, " I went up along the rise. You can see Alamosa from there. It don't look good, Billy. They started already. I seen torches moving out of town; high, like they were carried by men on horseback."

"Posse," Reo whispered.

Larnin's boots shifted. "You better let me take a look."

"The hell with the wound!"

Reo hauled himself to one elbow. The effort cost him plenty. There was a red-brown stain where his back had crushed the hay.

"What're the chances?" he said.

Larnin shook his head. "We got three, four hours on them, Billy. But we was riding too hard to cover trail. We left sign a blind man could follow."

Reo wet his lips. In the dark stillness now, a wind was rising and he could hear a voice praying high and shrill in Spanish and then cracking to dead silence.

Reo set his elbows, shoved himself erect. His teeth shut hard against the pain.

Larnin helped him. The numbness made his legs heavy and awkward. His insides burned. He held the pistol in a white-knuckled grip. He leaned against the wall, coughing for breath.

Larnin's face went uncertain. "Listen, Billy."

Pale eyes swung up. "I'm listening."

A minute passed. Their glances held. Then Larnin said, "Maybe it'd be better if you didn't run. You need a doctor, Billy. If you just waited here . . ."

"For the posse?" Reo said. "Sit here and wait for the mob to drag me out?" Fever made his stare too bright. "Wait for the rope?"

"I'm only saying . . ."

The gun hand lifted a fraction. "You said it. Now forget it."

"Sure, Billy, but . . ."

"But—you'd like to back down?"

"Billy, you got me wrong."

The gun was level with Larnin's belt buckle now. "Maybe," Reo said. "But you get me right. We're going to move. We're going to keep moving. They won't get me. Remember that, Jack. No mob'll ever get me."

Wind soughed in the stalls below. A rat skittered into the hay.

Larnin nodded. All he said was, "You still need a doctor."

"We'll head for Monte Vista. There's old Doc Carson."

Larnin frowned. "We ain't got much money. The doc mightn't want to . . ."

Billy Reo's hands moved light and smooth with the gun, broke it and checked the cylinder, snapped the breech shut again. He looked at the gun for a long time, then said, "He'll want to."

Shadows followed them. The moon was high and cloud-pierced and, behind them now, the pale meadows were restless with shadows that might have been wind bending the tall grass; or the groping movements of a posse.

Reo tried not to look back. Turned north and west toward the far reaches of the San Juan range, his face set rigid against thought and the memory of a sun bleached Panhandle town. The jogging of the saddle played hell with his back. He could feel the wounds seeping slowly; hot fingers clawed up from his belly and made breathing a torture.

Lifting gradually under them the land climbed toward distant foothills. The horses were wearing thin. The moon went down and winking stone-cold stars gave little light. Larnin took to shifting against the pommel, peering over his shoulder. Reo had drawn the Winchester from its saddle boot; he held it ready across his lap. Under the muffled dusty beat of hoofs, a Mexican tongue whimpered, *Madre de dios, socorro*, save me. *Madre de* . . .

"Shut up," Reo said aloud. "Shut up."

Larnin glanced at him sharply. A white edge fringed Reo's lips. He shook his head dully.

"Nothing. I was . . . Nothing."

Dawn was a pearl-grey cat paddling down from the westward mountains. A ground mist swirled rump-high to the ponies, made a cottony haze along the rim of Monte Vista. They reined in at the east end of the main street.

Reo felt dizzy. The numbness of his legs was worse.

"Jack. The poncho. In case we meet somebody."

Larnin unstrapped the latigoes and slipped the oilskin over Reo's shoulders. It hid the dark clotted stain of the shirt.

"All right," Reo said. "Let's go."

They didn't meet anybody. Monte Vista was curled up in sleep. A memory of stale beer and bought laughter drifted through dim saloon doorways. Even the red lights of the western skirt of town had gone dead. A dog hightailed across a side lane. Morning wind stirred the lazy dust.

The riders swung south along Don Paulo Street. Doc Carson's house was at the far end, grey, sand-eaten, set back in weeds. They hitched the ponies in the shelter of a sad willow and walked around to the kitchen door.

Reo moved slowly. Each step sent pain splintering through his chest and stomach. In the shade of the back stoop, he leaned against the wall, sucking deep lungsful of air. Larnin waited.

19

Finally, Reo said, "Now."

They didn't knock. The latch was up. The kitchen smelled of rancid coffee grounds. They went down the side hall. A thick, wet snoring led the way to the bedroom. Reo stopped on the doorsill. His palm rested lightly on the low-slung pistol.

The doc lay among crumpled quilts, fully dressed and booted. His string tie was undone and grey stubble matted his sunken cheeks. His mouth hung open. When he breathed out, a stink of whiskey tainted the air.

Reo made a sign. Larnin crossed to the window and drew the blind. In the dark now, Reo leaned at the foot of the bed. Larnin stood just beside the pillow. Reo nodded, Larnin lifted the Colt and pressed the small muzzle under the hinge of Doc Carson's jaw.

Long bony fingers knotted in the patchwork. The doc's eyelids twitched and opened very slowly.

"Quiet," Reo said. "Nice and quiet, Doc."

Carson sat up carefully, drawing back from the touch of the gun. "Reo. What is this?"

Reo set a smile against the biting twinges of the wound. "A professional visit, Doc."

Carson let out a long sigh, but he kept watching the gun. Some of the liquor-haze cleared from his eyes. "Law on your tail?"

The smile faded. "A misunderstanding," Reo said flatly. "There was a kid. He didn't trust me. I don't like it when people don't trust me."

The doc's stare wavered. The voice went shrill. "Well, what do you want with me? I can't . . ."

Reo turned around and pulled aside the poncho. Carson whistled, swung his feet to the floor. "Sit down," he said. "I'll look."

For a second, Reo didn't move. Finally, he sat on the bed.

Carson said, "I'll need light."

Larnin looked at Reo and then brought a lamp from the washstand and set fire to the wick.

The doc peeled off Reo's shirt. Flesh tore where flannel stuck to the edges of the wound. Reo sat still, head down, sweating. Carson's fingers prodded; his loose mouth pursed. He straightened.

Reo said, "So?"

Doc Carson scratched his jaw. "It won't be no cinch, Reo."

"You can do it?"

"There'll be a lot of pain."

Reo said, "You can do it."

The doc went to the clothes chest. He uncorked a bottle, drank and swabbed his mouth with a shirt sleeve. At last, he said. "This is against the law. I never handle these things, unless . . ."

Reo said, "You'll be paid."

A smile cracked wet lips. "Five hundred?"

Larnin's gun started to lift. "You lousy cheating . . ."

Reo shook his head. Larnin stood still. Reo looked at the doc.

"All right. Five hundred."

The smile broadened. Carson took a step forward.

"Not now," Reo said flatly. "Later. When this blows over."

21

Carson said, "Maybe you better get somebody else. I got nothing to ease the pain and . . ."

Abruptly, Reo stood up. His insides twisted and burned; nothing showed in his face. His hand hung over the thigh-thonged Colt. Carson went back a step.

"Like I told you," Reo said, "I don't like it when people won't trust me."

The lamp wick flickered. Morning was a pale yellow crack fringing the dark blind. Somewhere, a rooster crowed the day.

Doc Carson again tilted the bottle. The drink was a long one. He punched the cork home with his palm and said, "I'll get the instruments ready."

Reo sat down heavily. His head throbbed. He shut out the buzzing of his ears and looked up at Larnin. "Circulate," he said. "Ride out a ways. See if you can get wind of the posse."

Larnin flicked a glance at doc.

Reo said, "I'll handle him."

Carson kept working over his leather case. The instruments chinked as if his hands were trembling.

"How long?" Larnin asked.

Reo swung his gaze to Carson.

"An hour," Carson said. "Maybe two."

Reo's square blond face tightened. "That long?"

"I told you. Probing for that shot won't be no picnic."

Reo's breathing had picked up a beat. He managed to steady it and then he nodded at Larnin.

Larnin sheathed the gun and crossed to the hall. "I'll be back." The door closed.

The room was quite still. Reo could hear the rasp of his own lungs. He sat there, watching Carson spread bright tools on a towel on the bedside chair. Carson turned up the lamp wick and filled the washbasin with water from a cracked ewer. He rolled back his sleeves.

"On the bed," he said. "Belly down."

Reo sat still. Their eyes held. Reo drew the Colt and lay down, right arm stretched wide, the gun in his fist. His cheek pressed the greasy pillow, eyes turned toward the lamp. Carson's hands moved over the instruments, forced a thin wood splint against Reo's lips. "Bite when it gets bad." Carson lifted a needle-fine probe, bent over the bed. "This is it."

The probe went deep. The splint snapped between Reo's teeth.

They were coming. The posse was riding down on him and he could not move. He lay there, watching the hoofs rear and crash down at his face. They did not hang him at once. They drove white-hot pokers into his back and dragged him over live coals and then the rope burned his neck. He was praying in broken Spanish and the mob laughed when the knot jerked taut under his ear . . .

It lasted an hour and twenty minutes. Then the blackness went away. He could see the lamp, made pale now by the blaze of sun against the blind. The splint was gone. He tasted salt where his teeth had dug into the lower lip.

Stitches and plaster held him in a vise. Far off Monte Vista stirred with morning life. On the main drag, a pianola wrangled.

23

Doc Carson sat in the rocker by the window. "Sixteen buckshot," he was saying. "Don't know how you ever got this far."

Reo's lips burned. He licked them with a dry tongue. "Jack?"

"Yeah." Spurs chinked. "Here, Billy." Larnin brought him a tumbler of whiskey.

"Watch it," Carson said. "Watch them stitches."

Reo gained one elbow. His back seemed to tear apart, but the liquor helped. He looked up at Larnin. "Any luck?"

Larnin took the glass and refilled it. "If you'd call it that."

He drank. Reo waited.

"I was up to the saloon. Ran into this Express rider. He'd passed a party on the east road."

"And?"

"Posse," Larnin said. "Pony-boy says they was riding down a gunny. Lost his trail back in the meadows, then picked it up again. They're heading this way, Billy."

"How far behind are they?"

"Twenty miles when he saw them; moving slow, asking questions at every cabin they passed."

"Then we got time." Abruptly, Reo swung his legs out of bed. His mouth twitched with pain.

Doc Carson jumped up. "God A'mighty, man! Easy!"

Reo sat there, head low, hands clutching the mattress edge. "We ride," he told Larnin. "We make the mountains. They'll never track us through shale and rock."

Larnin said, "Billy, Maybe . . ."

"We won't go over that again," Reo said thickly. "We ride."

"Ride?" Carson shrilled. "Are you loco? Half an hour in the saddle and them stitches'll bust wide open. Your back'll be a sieve. And if you hemorrhage inwardly . . ."

Reo said, "Shut up."

"I tell you, it's one sure way to die."

Reo's mouth paled. "I can think of worse ways."

"But, my money . . ."

"Shut up!" Reo caught hold of the bedstead and rose very slowly. The room pitched wildly, but he did not fall. "I'll need a clean shirt, Doc."

It took a long while to get dressed. Finally, teeth set against a rising inward ache, Reo faced Larnin. "The horses?"

"All ready."

Reo lifted his pistol from the tangle of red-flecked covers. He turned to Carson. His eyes showed no emotion at all.

The doc's loose mouth went to pieces. "Listen, Reo." It was a dry whisper. "No hard feelings, eh? You know me. I'm a businessman. It ain't that I didn't trust . . ." Carson swallowed noisily and forced a smile. "Ain't that right, Reo? No hard feelings?"

"Yeah."

The gun went up fast and down. Carson saw it coming. He sidestepped too late. The barrel got him along the ear. He went down head first against the bed.

"Sure," Reo said softly. "No hard feelings."

Larnin wet his lips. "Look, Billy . . ."

The eyes stopped him. They were too brilliant and hard. "It gives us time," Reo said. "It'll remind him to keep his lip buttoned."

They went out through the kitchen. Reo waited in the warm shade of the stoop. Far up the street, a Mexican woman was stringing out wet wash. She did not look their way.

Larnin led the horses around. They had been fed and watered, but they didn't look rested. Reo frowned. There was no helping it. Trading for new mounts would only attract attention.

He caught the roan's stirrup and stepped up. The skin of his back stretched tight. Plaster cramped his ribs and he felt a wet ribbon run down his spine. He told himself it was only sweat, but he knew it was fresh blood. His jaw muscles corded. He gave Larnin the nod.

They rode along an alley to the south edge of town, then swung west. Reo sat with one hand resting on the butt of his Colt. Morning sun struck fire from the watchful slits of his eyes. They did not pass anybody. Far away, at the center of Monte Vista, a school bell chimed, clean and cool sounding.

When they hit open ground, Reo turned once. He saw the main drag, pale and dusty under a yellow sky. Wagons rumbled up with kegs from the brewery. Grangers lounged and smoked outside the barbershop and a fat woman waddled home with a basket of greens. There was no sign that anyone had noticed the passing of two strange riders.

The pain was a network of burning wires that jerked taut with every roll of the saddle. The wetness was thick along Reo's back now, soaking slowly into the bandages. He cursed Doc Carson for a bungler; he cursed a quick-tempered greenhorn and a man with a star pinned to his black vest. A nerve twitched his mouth.

"The hills," he said. "We make the hill and we're safe."

Larnin frowned. "It's a rough climb."

Reo seemed not to hear.

"We make the hills and we're all right," he said.

Larnin's frown deepened, but he didn't speak again.

Just before noon, they hit the first spur of the San Juans. Larnin hadn't been wrong. The going was steep and treacherous with tangleweed and shale. The horses didn't help. Reo's roan was whiteflanked and frothing at the bit. It walked head down, laboring against sun and the steady rise. Its feet were no longer sure.

Larnin was in the lead when they came onto the ledge. The pitching trail hung like the rungs of a ladder to the mountain face. The ledge was less than five feet wide with sheer wall to the left and, on the right, a drop of jagged rock to the next bench, thirty feet below.

Larnin heard the sudden slither of hoofs. Behind him, the roan shrilled and Reo yelled, "Jack!" He swung in the saddle, saw the roan already plunging over the rim, pawing for a grip. Reo twisted violently, trying to jump clear, but his right boot heel snagged the stirrup.

Man and horse went down together. Their screams echoed high above the rattle of shale, pierced the billow of rising dust. A few pebbles danced in their wake and the screaming stopped.

Larnin back-tracked on foot. It took time. Dust had settled; the lower bench lay still under the blistering sun. He saw the roan first. It had struck the ledge head-on; its neck was snapped and twisted at a foolish angle.

"Jack."

It wasn't more than a whisper. Reo lay against a boulder, legs stuck out straight before him, arms folded hard across his belly. The tear wasn't only skin-deep any more. There was a hot, wet feeling in his chest.

The grit-streaked face went crooked when Larnin tried to lift him. The legs wouldn't move at all. He tried to speak and the wetness welled into his throat. A bubble of red broke past his lips, trickled down into the blond beard. Larnin let go of him. Reo sat there, choking back the wetness, his eyes on Larnin. After a long time, he said, "So this is it."

Larnin did not answer. Uneasily now, his glance moved down the long ramp of the spur. He took a deep breath. "Listen Billy . . ."

The pale eyes didn't blink. "Go on. Say it."

Larnin's mouth worked. "I didn't have nothing to do with this, Billy. I never done no killing. We were friends. All right. I helped you while I could. But now . . ." The narrow jaw tightened. "Now I want out, Billy." He started to turn away.

"All right," Reo said. "You want out."

Larnin stared at the gun in Reo's fist. "Billy, you're crazy."

28

"I told you once. Whatever happened, it'd never be the posse. The mob'll never take me."

Slowly, the meaning got to Larnin. He shook his head. "I don't like it, Billy. I don't want your murder on my hands. You got a gun. You can do it yourself."

"Maybe," Reo said. "Only I can't be sure. It ain't easy to put a bullet through your own head. At the last minute, I might lose nerve." His gaze switched down to the blanched eastward flats. His voice went sharp. "Then they'd come with their goddam rope. They'd . . ."

It ended in a coughing fit. Bright red drained down his chin. The gun hand didn't waver.

"I'm not sure, Jack. You're going to do me a favor. You're going to make me sure."

"Billy . . ."

"That's how it is," The muzzle came belly-high on Larnin. "It's me or you, Jack."

They looked at each other. Then Larnin's bony fingers went down and closed on the Colt butt and the long barrel came up, clean and shining in the sun.

The posse came into Monte Vista at high noon. They rode wearily. Stetsons tilted against the glare, wetting grit-caked lips. The tall loose-limbed rider sat straight, scanning the dusty main street. The silver star winked against his black vest.

They were passing the telegraph office, when a man came running out. He wore a deputy's star. He waved a slip of yellow paper.

"You Rob Tucker? Sheriff down Alamosa way?"

The tall man nodded.

"Still riding the tail of that Reo fella?"

Tucker's eyes narrowed. "You got news?"

The man held out the yellow slip. "They sent that on for you. Said you'd pass this way, maybe want our help."

Tucker smoothed the paper on his thigh. Riders nudged close. "I'll be damned," Tucker said.

The deputy laughed. "That's what I says to my wife, 'That Reo's did it again.' Looks as if your hunting party's over, Sheriff. Seems like that Reckonridge boy is going to live, after all. Come to, early this morning, and said he wouldn't press any charges. Admitted he was starting to draw when Reo fired. Ain't much use arresting Reo when the victim hisself says it was self-defense." The grin widened. "Honest boy, that Reckonridge. Sounds like a nice kid."

"Yeah," Tucker said. "Nice kid."

The riders were silent, then something like a sigh of relief went among them. They hitched ponies and ambled off to the cool shade of the nearest saloon. Tucker dismounted and lit a cigarette. For a long moment, he stared at the match flame. He flung the match to the dust. "The luck of some sidewinders!"

The deputy nodded. "You had a long ride. You're wore thin."

"Can you figure it?" Tucker shook his head. "Here's this Reo, suspicioned of murder in four counties and just when we think he's pinned down, ready to bring to trial, out he slides by the skin of his teeth."

The deputy frowned. Then a thought made him smile.

"Say, I got some stuff up to the office. Curl the hair on your chest."

Tucker stared at the dead match. "The luck," he said. "The luck always rides with him." Then he shrugged and grinned back. "Like you say. It was a long ride."

They went off along the dry, hot boardwalk. The sheriff's office was at the east end of the main drag. Their backs were turned to the distant San Juan range. They didn't notice the shadows against the sun, the black, picket-winged birds that hovered for a long time above a mountain ledge and then circled down with a slow final grace.

WELL OF ANGER

By Morgan Lewis

Every once in a while, the editor of this anthology runs up against a character who is so impressive that, long after the story is read all the way through, the regret remains that the character isn't real so that he can be met personally and made a friend. As a kid, it was Doctor Doolittle; later on, Jeeves.

The hero of WELL OF ANGER is a character like that. He's a quiet, soft-spoken Quaker who never raises his voice, never cusses, and doesn't complain when he gets a pushing-around. But keep an eye on him when the necessity for getting tough really arises. . . .

JOE GATES put his paint cow pony through the creek and let him walk up the rise beyond. He was a tall, dark boy of fifteen, thin from overwork, and this day he had been in the saddle since sunup.

He could plainly hear the sound of Eliphalet Sawyer's ax and see its red gleam in dying light as the homesteader notched logs for his house. This camp, with its covered-wagon body on the ground for a tent, its cookstove under stretched canvas and the four big horses picketed nearby, was only a dot in the immensity of rolling range.

The man rested his double-bitted ax on the log as Joe came up. He was a pleasant young giant with merry blue eyes in a strong brown face fringed by a silky chestnut beard. He was naked to the waist and the light glinted on the curled hairs of his chest.

He wiped sweat from his forehead with a brown fore-arm and said, "How is thee, Joe?"

Joe wearily grinned and slumped sideways in the saddle. "Tired."

"The trouble still continues?"

The boy nodded unhappily. "This drought is givin' Gans his chance. We're busy every day hazin' back the stock that he drifts over onto us at night. With the range all burned to blazes, we need every bit of grass we've got."

Eliphalet considered this. "Why doesn't thy father talk to him?" he asked in his slow, deep voice.

Joe grinned wryly. "Talk to a knotheaded mule? When Luke Gans wants something he just goes after it an' there's no stoppin' him; he's got a tough crew to back him up."

The big man nodded, wiped his hands on his brown homespun pants and made two more cuts in the log.

"That is enough for today," he said, and rolled it across a litter of chips to the half completed walls of his house.

This was the first time Joe had seen him with his shirt off, and he marveled at the man's build and the way the great muscles slid under the milk-white skin. He no longer grinned at the man's speech, but he remembered when Eliphalet had first come to the ranch in early spring to tell pop that he had filed on land across the creek. Pop had been stiff—the land was open range, although they had always used it—but Eliphalet was so friendly and pleasant it was hard not to like him.

After he had gone, pop had said, "I reckon he's a Quaker. You took note of how he talked? I hear there's a settlement of 'em over beyond Dusty Forks. He must've struck out for himself."

That had been six months ago. Now Eliphalet had part of his land fenced and planted to corn and his house half up, but he had worked a full fourteen-hour day to do it.

He rested his ax against the logs, picked up a water jug and offered it to Joe.

"That creek water's too muddy," Joe said. "Why don't you get it from Big Spring?"

"I carried home a jugful last Sunday, but it does not last forever." Eliphalet's blue eyes twinkled. "Why did thy father build his house a mile from Big Spring?"

Joe grinned. "He'd have started a war if he'd tried to take Big Spring—it's on open range. . . . Say, mom wants you for dinner tomorrow. It's Sunday, in case you've forgot."

"Thy mother is kind, Joe. Thank her for me." Eliphalet tilted the jug to his lips, and muscles writhed in his awesome arms.

"Gee-e-e." Joe made the word long drawn out. "You're built like—like a bull."

The big man lowered the jug and wiped his mouth with the back of his hand. "Muscles are not everything, Joe. It is what a man carries in his heart and his head that counts."

"Maybe," Joe said, "but if I had muscles like yours I'd catch Luke Gans alone sometime and break him in little pieces." His two hands showed exactly how it should be done. "Well"— he gathered the reins—"I need sleep. See you tomorrow."

34

Riding the mile to the ranch, he drowsily thought of Eliphalet and his strength. Why, there wasn't a man in the county that would be able to stand up to him in a fight. It made him feel good to have a friend like that. It gave him a feeling of confidence and safety.

Abby had on her new brown dress for dinner. She was just nineteen; and her hair was black, and curled softly like ma's. Joe noticed how bright her dark eyes were when she looked across the table at Eliphalet.

He tremendously admired the Quaker's table manners. Not once did Eliphalet put his knife in his mouth, and he was nice and polite and bragged up everything he ate. When ma said a certain thing had been cooked by Abby, he bragged it even more, until the color came up into Abby's smooth cheeks.

"You know," Joe said in a wondering tone, "we were out this morning and there wasn't a head of Gans' stock on our range."

"Prob'bly giving us a day off to rest up," pop said with grim humor. He was dark and lean, with the beginning of a bald spot at the crown of his black head. He had worked hard with rope and saddle all his days and his shoulders under the blue shirt were slightly stooped.

"I do not see," Eliphalet said gravely, "why a man should want land that belongs to another. Has he not range of his own?" Joe liked to hear him talk. He used words kind of funny, different from the folks hereabout.

Pop gripped the fork upright in his dark fist. "You ever see a rancher figured he had enough?" Pop shook his head.

"He's big and he wants to be bigger; he wants to be king. He's already crowded out a couple of two-bit ranchers on the other side. One of 'em," he said slowly, "was kind of weak-kneed. Gans went in and slapped him around until he was glad to quit."

"He beat him?"

"Well," pop said, "the feller's wife did the drivin' when they left. He wasn't in any condition to see."

"Now, John," ma said reprovingly, "you promised there wouldn't be any talk of trouble. Can't you forget Luke Gans for just a minute?"

"I'd be glad to," pop said, "if he'd forget me."

Joe knew what he meant. Gans was the kind that never let up. If one thing failed, he would try another, and each thing he did would be tougher. Pop never rode out, now, without his Colt at his hip and a rifle in the saddle boot. The thought sent coldness through him and ruined his appetite, until ma brought in the pie.

It was surprising the easy way Eliphalet fitted into the family. The first time ma had invited him pop had objected, because he was opposed to nesters, but ma had said, "It is hard for a young man to live alone. It wouldn't be Christianlike not to ask him."

Since then he had been here almost every Sunday, but he wasn't pushing and never came unless invited. And he always brought fresh vegetables from his garden, riding up on one of his big plow horses with a blanket for saddle.

Toward evening he and Abby took his jug and walked the mile downslope to Big Spring. Pop had gone to sleep, slumped down in his big chair, his rope-hardened hands crossed on his flat stomach.

Joe wandered out to the porch where ma had gone for a breath of air. He was idly watching the tiny figures at the spring when a man topped a rise and rode toward it.

Even at this distance something struck him as familiar, and he got the glasses. "Ma," he said, taking a deep breath, "Luke Gans is down at the spring!"

Ma looked nervously into the room where pop slept. "Don't wake your father," she said. "After all, the spring is on open range; he has as much right there as we have."

"Well," Joe said, "I'll go see what he wants, anyway." He went out to the corral and got his horse. Riding down, he thought confidently, *If Gans tries to push Eliphalet around, he'll get his head knocked off*. The thought did him a world of good and he was feeling fine when he reached the spring.

Luke Gans was a square, blocky figure in overalls and checked shirt with a red bandanna around his neck. He sat his big bay like a rock, quirt dangling from wrist, and the bay's nose was not six inches from Eliphalet's face.

As Joe arrived, Eliphalet grasped the reins close under the bay's chin and forced him back. "There is room for thy horse, friend," he said mildly, "without seeking the ground where I stand."

Gans' heavy face went a brick red and his stone-gray eyes flared. "Let loose my bridle, you damned nester!" he yelled. He leaned forward in the stirrups and brought the heavy quirt down with a full-arm swing.

Joe's stomach congealed; it became a solid lump of ice that crowded against his heart and took his breath. The lash cut across Eliphalet's shoulder and back, and its sound blended with Abby's scream.

For a moment the Quaker's big body swayed. He took a step forward, his fists knotted like hammers. *Ah,* Joe thought, *Gans picked on the wrong man this time; Eliphalet will haul him off his horse and beat him to a pulp.* A sudden wave of savagery swept through him. "Smash him!" he said, and did not recognize his own voice.

But Eliphalet paused. A deep breath ran out of him and his hands loosened. "There was no need for that, friend," he said in a shaken voice.

"Keep your hands off my bridle," Gans said, "or you'll get more!" His eyes flicked to Abby. "That's the way to handle nesters." He settled his big hat on his head and rode off.

Abby made a small, stifled sound. She looked with eyes strained wide at Eliphalet. She saw the red line where the quirt had cut seeping through his shirt, and her white hands balled at her breast. "He struck you," she said in a small voice, "and you did nothing—nothing!" Her face worked, but her eyes were bright and dry. "He beat you with a whip! What—what kind of a man are you?" Her voice broke on the last word, and she turned away and walked upslope through the slanting red light with bent head.

Eliphalet made a half gesture with his hand and let it drop. He stared without sound after Abby, and his face was the saddest Joe had ever seen.

38

And then embarrassment touched Joe. He could no longer bear to look at him. He turned his horse and rode after his sister. Going home, shadows, like hungry wolves, ran swiftly over the land. He felt vast loneliness and fear. He had witnessed the destruction of an idol and the full measure of Gans' brutality. Long after he was in bed he heard Eliphalet come slowly to the house, get his big horse and ride off into the night.

When Joe went by Big Spring next morning, the jug was still there, smashed against a rock where some careless hoof had knocked it. The glittering pieces were trampled into the mud.

It was three days before Joe could bring himself to ride down to the homestead. But he had to see Eliphalet; he had to know. It was as though a death had occurred in the ranch house. Mom was unusually quiet, and Abby went about her work, tight-lipped. Mornings her eyes were red, as though she had not slept. There was a solid, heavy weight in Joe's stomach.

The paint pony splashed through a shallow pool in the practically dry creek bed and went slowly up the other side. Joe had to see the big Quaker, but he dreaded it.

The house was no further along than when he had last seen it and, for a moment, he thought Eliphalet had gone. Then he saw the well. It was near the house and not deep, but water flowed in it clear and bright. Gee, Eliphalet was lucky. Pop had gone down twenty feet for their well.

Eliphalet came around the corner, and Joe felt shocked. He was worn and haggard looking and the merriment had gone from his blue eyes. They seemed to have deepened and grown darker.

Joe slid off his horse and stood, feeling young and awkward.

"Still working hard, Joe?" the big man asked.

He shook his head. "Hasn't been a Gans steer on the place since last Sunday. I can't understand it." Then the question that had been yeasting inside him came out with a rush, "Gee, why did you take it? Why didn't you come back at him?"

Eliphalet dragged a sleeve across his face. He said in a dull voice, "Friends do not believe in fighting."

"Friends?" Joe's voice was scornful. "Gans hasn't got a friend in the world."

"The Society of Friends," Eliphalet explained wearily. "They do not believe in laying hands on a man in violence."

Joe stared. Pop had said something about this, but Joe hadn't taken much stock in it. Now he was confronted by the stark reality of a man who didn't believe in fighting. "But—but s'pose somebody takes a swing at you?"

" 'A soft answer turneth away wrath.' "

"Well, gee——" Joe was confused. You couldn't very well argue with the Bible, but something was wrong. "It didn't turn away Gans' wrath. Don't you see," he argued desperately, "there's times when you just have to poke a fella in the nose?"

Eliphalet sighed. "That is true; there are times when anger takes thee by the throat and reason departs. Later thee is sorry, but the harm is done." He gazed off into the distance where Dry Forks lay hidden by the earth's bulge, and Joe got the feeling he was far removed from this time and place.

"It's tough out here," Joe said. "Pop says so, and I reckon he's right. Why, if a fella doesn't stand up for himself, every saddle bum in the country will cuff him around."

"Thee has thy way, Joe," the big man said, "and I have mine." There was a finality in his voice that shut off further discussion. "Tomorrow I start drawing firewood from the hills. I will bring thy father a load."

Joe nodded and stepped into the saddle. He rode home with the weighty feeling still in his stomach.

Joe raced his pony in off the range just before noon as Eliphalet was unloading his wood. "Hey, pop!" he yelled. "Pop! Gans is fencing; he's coming right down the line!"

Pop turned from helping Eliphalet and a surprised, pleased look came over his face. "I've always hated bob-wire," he said, "but this is one time I'm glad to see it go up."

Eliphalet dragged the last pole from the wagon and let it drop. "This means he will leave thee in peace?"

Pop nodded. "No other reason for him to fence. Now his stock won't keep driftin' over onto us. It must be," he said slowly, as though trying to figure it out, "that he's decided we're too tough and has quit. He——"

Pop broke off as a sound came faintly like a far-off shot. It came again and again, the sound of shots . . .or of someone pounding. He swung on his heel and strode around the house.

When Joe came up with him he was staring downslope. A crew of three men had moved in by Big Spring and were driving posts. Even without glasses Joe could see that they were fencing the spring. In back of them was a wagon loaded with fence posts.

Pop said in a bleak, bitter voice, "I should've known better than to think Gans would quit."

"Is not Big Spring on thy land?" Eliphalet asked, beside him.

Pop's face was grim. "Open range," he said. "We've both used it. Now that the water holes are dry and the creek's run out, he figures to grab it and put me over a barrel."

"This means no water for thy stock?"

"None at all," pop said. "There's just one way to fix this."

He went into the house. When he came out he was carrying the rifle. Joe watched in a kind of tight fascination as he methodically shoved shells into it.

"Thee is not going to shoot men in cold blood!" Eliphalet protested.

"You tend to your business, Sawyer," pop said, "and I'll tend to mine." He shoved in the last shell.

Eliphalet was sweating. He said, "But that would be murder. There are other ways——"

Pop gave him a level look. "You didn't do so well the other night." He bellied down on the ground.

Joe breathed shallowly off the top of his lungs as he

watched the rifle steady. This was bad trouble; it had never come to shooting before.

Two men were riding up on the left but pop paid them no heed; he leveled the rifle at the men down by the spring and pulled trigger.

The three jumped apart and wheeled as the top post on the loaded wagon jumped and skittered off. Pop levered in another shell and dust spurted a yard from the man with the sledge. He jumped again, dropped his sledge and ran for the wagon.

And then a shout arose from the two riders and they spurred toward the house. Pop stood up, rifle cradled in his arm. "Look at him run." There was vast contempt in his voice.

Joe turned. He hadn't seen Eliphalet leave. Now the Quaker was on one of his big horses, heading for his homestead. He had kicked the animal into a lumbering run.

"That boy smells trouble," pop said, "and he doesn't want any part of it." He shrugged. "Well, no fight of his," and turned as the two horsemen pounded into the yard.

Joe's throat went suddeny dry—Luke Gans and Sheriff Bob Merrill, of Dusty Forks. The sheriff said, "Howdy, Gates." He was a small compact man with eyes as arresting as gun muzzles.

Pop just nodded, his eyes flicking from the sheriff to Gans, sitting smugly in the saddle.

"Doing a little target practice?" Merrill was noted for never raising his voice; his reputation with a gun made it unnecessary.

"Just settin' my sights on the spring," pop said.

"Don't do it again," Merrill said quietly. "Gans' fore-man, Boots Hardy, has filed homestead rights there."

Pop sucked in his breath. He was stunned for a moment. Then fury flooded into his face and he swung on Gans. "You robber!" he yelled. "You're out to steal my water!"

Merrill kicked his horse between them. "You can fight all you please over free range, Gates," he said, "but Hardy's filed legally. I'll have to back him up."

Pop's hands clenched, but he was licked. Gans had made a move that put the sheriff on his side, and there wasn't a man in the country that would shoot it out with him.

"I reckon," Gans drawled, "now you'll be tame as your Quaker friend."

Pop was breathing hard. He said, "Get off that horse and I'll quick show you different."

Gans just grinned and wheeled his horse.

"I'm sorry," Merrill told pop. "It isn't a job I like, but that's the way it is." He rode after Gans. The two men conferred, then the sheriff headed back for town and Gans went on down to the spring.

Pop stared after them and the look on his face fright-ened Joe. Never before had pop looked beaten. He had taken the worst of his troubles with chin up, but now his shoulders sagged and the lines of his face were deeper cut. Years of hard, bitter work were being swept away by one man's greed. His stock could not live without water. Joe remembered seeing a disabled steer die of thirst, and shuddered.

The pounding resumed down at the spring and Joe felt a new, dreadful fear. Pop was desperate; that sound would

44

drive him crazy. His big hands were clamping the rifle until the knuckles showed white. He might lose his head and start shooting.

"Pop," Joe faltered. "Pop——" And then he heard the pound of hoofs and saw Eliphalet returning, the big horse lathered. "Hey, pop," he said loudly, "here's Eliphalet back!" and felt deep relief at this break in the tension.

Eliphalet slid off beside them. "Thee has failed, John Gates? They are taking thy spring?"

Pop didn't answer, but there was a smoldering light in his black eyes. "They've homesteaded Big Spring," Joe explained. "Gans got the sheriff to side him."

Eliphalet nodded, as though not surprised. "That is wrong. It may be within the law, but it is wrong." He dragged air into his deep chest. "We will have to steal it back for thee."

Pop gave him a bitter, impatient glance. "Sure, we'll just hook on block 'n' tackle and haul it up on my land."

Eliphalet said in a steady voice, "If I get thy spring back, will thee promise there will be no shooting?"

Pop had started to turn away. Now, at the sincerity in the big man's voice, he swung back. He put his eyes on Eliphalet and he studied the big brown face. "Sawyer, if you can get that spring back, I'll throw away my gun— that's a promise. But I don't reckon you can."

"Thee will see," Eliphalet said calmly. . . . "Joe, fetch spade and crowbar."

That's queer equipment to steal a spring with, Joe thought as he loped off. He slowed at the house, where ma stood in the doorway, hands nervously clasped over her apron. "Hey, we're going' to steal Big Spring back!" he informed her.

Ma turned into the room. "Abby," she said quickly, "go with them. They are less apt to start trouble with a woman along."

But there was no sign of Abby when Joe got back to the wagon. He threw tools onto the sideless floor boards and sat sideways beside pop, with his legs dangling.

"How far down the slope does thy land lie?" Eliphalet asked as they jolted along.

Pop pointed to a narrow bench that broke the slope a hundred yards from the spring. "Far side of that bench."

Gans and his crew came into clearer sight as the wagon rolled closer. They already had a section of posts set and the wire strung.

"Not wasting any time," pop said grimly.

Eliphalet stopped the team on the level land and got down. "Wait here," he said, and strode on down to the fence. Joe saw him take a slender forked stick from his boot top.

Gans and his crew stared curiously, but Eliphalet paid them no heed. He took the two ends of the stick in his hands with the point of the v pointing toward his body, and moved along the fence. Opposite the spring he turned and came upslope, not straight, but on a diagonal, as though some invisible force were guiding him. He came up onto the bench and across it. Where the slope resumed, the stick bent in his big hands and pointed down.

"A water dowser," pop murmured wonderingly. "I've heard tell of 'em, but I never took much stock."

Eliphalet ground his heel into the earth and shoved the stick back into his boot. "Here is thy spring," he said.

Joe took a deep, quavery breath of pure excitement. This he would have to see. He lugged spade and crowbar over to the spot and Eliphalet started to dig. He was still scooping out topsoil when Abby stopped her horse beside them.

A red blouse was tucked into her divided skirt and her hair was plaited and wound about her head against the jar of riding. She sat her horse and watched, a coolly impersonal look in her eyes.

Eliphalet met her glance. He nodded and kept on digging, but Joe saw color seep into his neck. He worked steadily while the sweat began to roll off him. At hardpan he used the bar to pry chunks of it loose.

"Let me take a turn at that," pop said, and Eliphalet climbed out, the wet shirt clinging to his great shoulders, and watched while pop dug. Presently he took his stick and approached the hole at right angles. "About four feet down," he said.

Joe had distinctly seen the wood writhe and bend. He reached out with a grin and took it, but in his hands it was just a piece of dead wood.

"Some have the power, and some have not," the Quaker told him gravely.

Pop continued to dig, working furiously, grunting with each shovelful, and Joe felt his driving excitement as the hole grew deeper. Abby maintained her cool look, but the little pulse in her throat, that showed when she was angry or excited, was throbbing.

47

Pop stopped for a breath and Eliphalet took over. Pop got out and stood on the edge, breathing heavily. Wet hair was plastered on his forehead and he had skinned a knuckle on the rough side wall.

Presently, as the hole went deeper, a tiny doubt crept into Joe's mind. There was no sign of water, not even a slight muddiness. The ground was hard and dry, as though the drought had baked clear down into it. Aw, how could a man trace water underground with just a little stick anyway?

Pop said in a skeptical voice, "You're past four feet now."

Eliphalet climbed out. Water ran from him and his face was dark red. He took the stick and came to the hole again, moving it from side to side, watching it closely. Then he jumped back into the hole, whirled the bar overhead and drove it deep into a corner.

Water spouted as though he had knocked the cork from a jug and Joe whooped. He struck again and again, enlarging it, and water gushed in a steady flow. Before he climbed out, it was swirling almost to his boot tops.

Pop stared with unbelieving eyes. "An' all the time," he murmured, "it was on my land, if I'd known how to find it!"

And then Joe gave another whoop at this sudden breaking of strain. He capered on the edge of the new spring and whooped like an Indian while Abby's horse danced in excitement.

Gans' crew stopped their work to stare, and Gans, struck by a sudden thought, walked over to Big Spring.

"Thee had best leave," Eliphalet said, "and give tempers a chance to cool."

Pop stared. "Why? I don't see——"

Eliphalet jerked a thumb toward the fence. "His spring is gone." He turned and started downslope.

Pop slapped his leg. "Well, I'll be —— Wait a minute, boy. I'll go with you."

Eliphalet turned. He shook his head. "Remember thy promise, John Gates." His glance rested on the Colt at pop's hip. Then he went striding down the slope, his big boots kicking dust from the grass.

Joe looked at pop for permission, got his worried nod and loped after Eliphalet, but his eyes went beyond the big man and across the fence.

Gans had made his discovery, and now turned, his face black and bonehard with anger. He came toward the fence as Eliphalet approached from the other side, and Joe felt a dryness in his mouth. The Quaker had made a fool of the rancher before his crew. Gans had gone to the trouble of having his foreman file and fence on dry ground.

Eliphalet paused and said, "We have taken thy spring, but there is——"

Gans gave a great yell, as though his anger was too great to contain. He ran at the fence and put his hands on it and came over in a leap. He had been blocked, and that was the one thing his arrogant nature could not stand. He ripped his overalls on a barb and a flap hung down as he came at Eliphalet. He was cursing steadily in a crazy kind of voice.

Fright yelled through Joe. Eliphalet wouldn't fight; this

man would beat his face off; he would kill him. "Look out!" he yelled, his voice a thin bleat of fear.

And then Gans reached his man and aimed a great, sweeping blow at the head. Eliphalet swayed away from it, but the rancher's hard-knuckled fist plowed along the side of his face. He staggered, took another blow on his arm, then his hands shot out. Twice he slapped Gans, open-handed, once on either side of the face, with full-arm swings. They cracked with a heavy, meaty sound.

The blows stopped Gans and dazed him so that he swayed on his feet like a sledged steer. Eliphalet bent forward and clamped his hands on the man's hips. The shirt split down his back as he lifted Gans over his head. He took five steps, said, "Thee has no business on this side, friend," and pitched him over the fence.

Gans struck on his back, and the wind went out of him with a deep rushing sound. He lay in the dust under downpouring sunlight, and the color washed out of his face, leaving it gray. Presently he slowly rolled on his side and drew up his knees. The effort to get breath into his lungs made a deep groaning.

Wire pinged as Eliphalet went over the fence. He knelt beside Gans and helped him to sit up. "Twice thee struck me," he said. "Once with the whip and once with the fist; it was more than mortal flesh could endure."

Joe stared. This was a queer ending to a fight. He looked sideways at the idling crew and saw them exchange glances. The man with the sledge spat on his hands and went back to work.

Joe was still wondering when Eliphalet helped Gans to

his feet and the two walked off along the fence. Eliphalet again had the forked stick in his hands. Joe turned and went slowly uphill. The big man's actions sorely puzzled him. It now looked as though he were finding water for Gans.

Pop was standing by the wagon, an uncertain, irritable look on his face. But there was nothing uncertain about Abby. She stood by her horse, her eyes shining and her lips softly parted. Joe sat on the wagon and waited.

When Eliphalet came, he moved slowly, as though this day had wearied even his great strength. He was dirty and sweaty; his torn shirt hung loosely upon him, and Gans' fist had left a red streak along his face. He said, "I have found Gans a spring."

Pop shook his head. "I don't understand. Now the trouble will begin all over again; we're right back where we started."

"No," Eliphalet said, "no. There will be no more trouble. Luke Gans' new spring also arises on thy land."

Pop stared. Then, as the full significance came to him, the worry and the look of pressure left his face. He made a halfturn away from Eliphalet and swung back. "It's a small thing to say I'm obliged, Sawyer." He took a deep breath. "I give you my word I'll never shut him off from water so long as he acts decent. I reckon that's what you want?"

Eliphalet nodded. He looked down at his big hands. "Once before, in Dusty Forks, a man raised his hand against me and I struck him to the ground. The Society put me on probation, and now I have again laid violent hands on a man." He shook his head. "In some the flesh is stronger than the spirit. It takes long for a man to know himself, to find where his course lies." There was hint of sadness in his voice.

And then Abby left her horse and came to him. "Is that such a bad thing?" she asked. There was a warm, bright light in her eyes, and she stood directly before him.

He looked at her steadily, but her eyes did not drop and their light seemed to grow and spread until it touched him and he smiled.

"Why, no," he said. "It is not bad at all."

Pop touched Joe's arm and they went over to Abby's horse, but all he said was, "Joe, I reckon this horse will have to carry double."

As Joe swung up behind him he heard Abby say, "I haven't seen your house yet, Eliphalet."

At the top of the slope he looked back. The wagon was rolling toward the log house set in the new planting, and Abby's red blouse was a bright, hopeful spot of color.

TWO-FACED PROMISE

By Bill Gulick

TWO-FACED PROMISE is a yarn typical of the real-life frontier—the story of a man with a job to do and enough faith
to do it despite any and all obstacles. In this case, the job
is to get a railroad through, and the obstacles would easily
stop a lesser man: an indifferent Congress, the necessity
for taking an Indian chief's word that a pass exists in un-
explored territory, and a member of the party found with
an arrow in his back.

Captain Thaddeus Bradley, engineer in charge of the
survey party, was in his tent writing a letter to his wife
when the lanky, saturnine-faced, Steve Conners, appeared
in the entryway and said, "The Indians are waiting."

Captain Bradley laid aside his pen, donned his hat and
followed the scout across the camp to where the saddled
horses waited. Mounting, they forded the shallow river
and rode across an open park where the grass grew rich
and green, Conners slouching loose and relaxed in the saddle, Bradley holding his short, stocky figure stiffly erect
to ease the dull throb of pain in his right side. It was nearly
noon. The late September sun stood straight overhead,
warm even at that high altitude, and veiling cedar and pine
on the upper slopes of the foothills in a translucent haze.
Silence rode with the two men for a while, then the captain
said, "Can we trust him?"

"Maybe." Conners lifted his shoulders in a shrug. "Chief

53

Qualchee is an educated Indian. Mission school. But that doesn't guarantee anything. Some Indians don't learn to lie till white men teach 'em." The scout gave Bradley a quizzical look. "How does he strike you?"

The captain considered for a moment. Problems of engineering could be measured by the tangible yardstick of facts, but long ago he had learned that men must be measured by less tangible things—a gesture, a tone of voice, a quiet glitter of the eye.

He said slowly, "A man who has the best interests of his people at heart."

"That," Conners said dryly, "puts us right back where we were."

"You think the only feasible pass is to the southwest?"

"It's big country. I could be wrong."

The implication was clear enough: there might be other passes through the mountain range to westward, but Conners did not regard it as likely. The captain knew that Conners was a man whom years in the West had taught caution. That was at once a virtue and a fault. The captain's thoughts started circling again, like a terrier chasing its own tail. The final decision must be his own. The matter resolved itself to this: Either Chief Qualchee was to be trusted or he was not. It was as simple and yet as difficult as that.

Thaddeus Bradley was a man driven by a single dream. For years he had fought an indifferent Congress, a skeptical President and an openly hostile Secretary of War in a stubborn and continuing battle to make that dream a reality—and in the end he had won the grudging victory of a small appropriation and a commission to lead a survey party westward from Saint Paul to Puget Sound. The money was spent now and no hope of getting more. The men were weary and disgruntled. He was tired. An old injury suffered in the Mexican War had returned to plague him and make every minute in the saddle torture, but the job was nearly done. With the early mountain winter weeks away, only a single rugged range lay between the party and its goal. But railroads did not climb mountains. Somewhere there had to be a pass, a low, gentle grade relatively free of snow, or the entire survey was worthless.

He thought of the commission which had been given him months before. ". . . empowered to search out the most feasible northern route for a railroad to the West, to treat with the Indian tribes encountered and set aside lands for them to the end that permanent peace may be insured . . ." It was a bit of irony that the only known pass through the mountains lay in a country jealously claimed by one of the strongest Indian tribes in the West. Well, the wording of the commission made the choice simple. The railroad came first; peace, second.

The Indians were camped at the edge of the park a few miles south of the river. Chief Qualchee waited, a tall impassive man whose dignity clothed his powerful body with a quiet grace that no white man's raiments could ever have achieved. Dismounting, Captain Bradley studied him as they went into the council lodge, seated themselves and commenced the long ceremony of pipe-smoking which always preceded important discussions, trying to read whatever truth was in him.

"You brought the paper?" the Indian said at last, staring straight at Bradley.

"I have it here in my hand. Do you wish it read to you?"

Qualchee waved it away. "The white man's words always stand on straight legs but sometimes the hand that writes them lies."

"My words and my hand are one."

The Indian inclined his head slightly. "Good. Then the bargain is done. South of where the river runs—this shall be our land, as it always has been. When the beast that spits fire comes, it will not eat out land. It will turn northward and cross the mountains at the place I have agreed to show you."

"There is a pass to the northwest?"

"I have said it."

Captain Bradley's eyes went to Conners' face, and found it stony, expressionless. Whom was a man to believe? A white scout who admitted that his knowledge of the country was limited? A partly civilized savage who might best serve his people by lying?

He said quietly, "We will sign the treaty."

They had recrossed the river and were riding into camp before Conners spoke. His eyes probed the irregular horizon line to the northwest. "Winter comes early in the mountains. If the pass ain't there, there'll be no turning back."

The jolting of the saddle had made the pain in Captain Bradley's side start throbbing again, a pulsing, tearing pain that forced him to breathe in shallow gasps. "I know," he said shortly.

He called the men together and spoke to them briefly. "I've signed the treaty. From now on the land south of the river belongs to the Indians. I want no trespassing—for any reason. Qualchee has promised to join us tonight. We'll start for the mountains tomorrow."

Afterwards, he went to his tent and rested on his cot for an hour. When the pain had lessened somewhat, he arose and went back to the unfinished letter to his wife, which he planned to give to the expected army dispatch rider from the east who was due that afternoon. He read over what he had written, then picked up his pen.

. . . . I signed the treaty with the Indians today. Perhaps it was a mistake. I'm sure Conners thinks so and I'm sorry for that, for he is the only man in the party who seems to be in sympathy with what I am trying to do. It was not an easy decision to make. If the best pass lies in Indian country south of the river, then that is the route the railroad should take—even if it means war. But the die is cast. Qualchee says that there is an easier and better pass to the northwest. I am risking the success of the entire project on the supposition that he is a man of honor. If his word is good. . . .

He heard a horse clatter into camp and the voices of men raised in greeting. A moment later the dispatch rider, a slight, wiry figure with dust powdering the blue of his faded uniform, appeared in the doorway of the tent. He saluted, then handed the captain a packet of letters.

"You'll start back as soon as you eat?" Captain Bradley said.

"I'll wait till dark. Too many Indians around to suit me."

"They're peaceful."

"Perhaps, sir. But I'll still wait till dark."

Captain Bradley thumbed quickly through the letters, putting aside those from his wife and saving them until he had finished what was bound to be more unpleasant reading. The official letters contained the usual complaints. The government would honor no more drafts for supplies and pack animals and he would be held personally responsible for any further debt incurred. Sentiment in Congress was changing, swayed by the fiery, eloquent Secretary of War, Jefferson Davis, who, being a Southerner, favored the southern transcontinental route for the railroad. It was thought that a compromise might be reached and a central route through the Rockies decided upon. This, Captain Bradley thought angrily, despite Fremont's abysmal failure to penetrate those mountains in his expedition of a few years ago!

A shadow filled the tent doorway and he looked up to see the thick figure of George Joslyn, one of the party's civilian teamsters. "What is it?" the captain said impatiently.

Joslyn was a heavy, morose man, slow of thought and action, a man drawn into himself by a secret dream that set him apart from the others. He did the job he was paid to do but no more; whatever free time he had to himself he spent in pursuing the will-o'-the-wisp of his private dream. That dream was gold.

As part of his personal effects, he had brought along from Saint Paul a miner's pan, a pick and a short shovel, and each time the party crossed a likely looking stream he somehow found time to dig a few shovelsful of sand, squat by the water's edge and test it. The other men had been interested at first, then, as his efforts showed little results and they learned the unpleasant fact that prospecting for gold was hard work, the interest gave way to amusement, and, finally, to indifference — none of which affected George Joslyn in the least. He continued to search, to dig, to dream.

There had been a time when Captain Bradley had cherished the hope that Joslyn would make a strike. Gold would bring people west. Gold would assure the success of the northern railroad route. Gold would pay the mounting deficit of the survey party—a deficit which now promised to make him a pauper. But time was running out, and the only gold he sought now was the hope that somewhere to the northwest he would find the vital pass.

"Captain," Joslyn said with blunt directness, "I'm quitting. I'm not going on with the party."

"The word," Bradley said quietly, "is deserting."

"Call it what you want, I'm through."

"You have a reason, I suppose?"

"If I do, it's my own affair."

Bradley gazed up at the man, trying to read what lay behind the uncomfortable expression in the heavy face. At last he said, "I'm busy now, Joslyn. I'll talk to you later."

His face was troubled for a moment after the man had

gone, then it softened as he opened the letters from his wife, letters written months before and a wide continent away. They were cheerful letters for the most part, but here and there a phrase crept in that brought worry to his eyes.

. . . . a hard winter here in Massachusetts. The snow still lies in the hill pasture and feed for the cattle is scarce . . . Esther has a bad cough. I'm sure it will be all right when spring comes, but, oh, it's so long in coming . . .

He looked up from the letter and his eyes found the mellow sunlight sparkling on the clear surface of the river and the lovely park beyond. He thought of the vast, empty stretches of fertile park and meadow and wide reach of plain he had crossed since leaving Saint Paul, good land needing only the touch of the plow to make it productive. Then he thought of the bleak New England hills where he had been born and the stone-cluttered valleys where farmers tilled so frugally during the few months of the growing season. Tired, worn-out, sour land.

He sat for a long while gazing out across the camp, then he picked up the pen and started writing again.

The dispatch rider just brought half a dozen letters from you. I can't tell you how welcome they are. Though I know you're doing your best to conceal it, I can sense that you're worried and discouraged. I know the farm is poor. I know it's hard to live on what little money I am able to send you, but if you can bear up a little while longer my

*job here will be done, then I will come for you. You ask
if this is not a terribly lonely land. At the moment it is,
my dear, but it will not be long. When the railroad is built
—as it surely will be—the people will come and the land
will prove fruitful as that of the East never has. This is
land of great promise . . .*

He wrote steadily on while the afternoon sun moved
slowly across the sky toward the jagged blue line of peaks
on the western horizon.

An hour before sunset he stopped writing and got up
and went out of the tent. Men sprawled about the camp,
dozing and talking and waiting hungrily while the cook
prepared the evening meal. Seeing Conners, the captain
said, "Has Qualchee come?"

"No."

"He promised to be here by dark."

"What's his promise worth?"

So Conners has lost faith too. The feeling of being com-
pletely alone made the captain look at the scout with a
rising anger, then the anger died and became resigned
acceptance. No words could inspire faith when the will-
ingness to believe was gone. "Have you see Joslyn?" he
said shortly.

"Couple of hours ago. He was headin' toward the river
with his pick an' shovel an' pan. Guess he's gone pokin'
around in the hills."

Captain Bradley frowned. He walked down to the river
and stood on the north bank for a time, thinking of Joslyn

and his morose, stubborn dream. Growing apprehension came to him. He picked his way across the river on the flat boulders, searched for a moment along the south bank and presently found the clear, deep print of a boot in the moist sand. His sign. It led south across the park, south into forbidden land toward the rising foothills, which were turning blue now with growing dusk.

"The fool!" he muttered. "The damned fool!"

He found George Joslyn just as the last pale glow of daylight was fading from the sky. He found him in the bend of a stream a few miles south of the river—lying still and unmoving on his face with the chill water gurgling around him and an Indian hunting arrow protruding from the center of his back. He had not been dead long, for his body was not yet stiff, but the quiet murmur of the stream, the still rustle of pine on the slope above, told no tales of how he had died or whose hand had bent the bow.

Captain Bradley turned the body over on its side, staring with fascination at the sharp, barbed point protruding from beneath the breast bone and the red, green and white feathers bound to the arrow's notched end. He stood up. Near-by lay the pick, the shovel and the miner's pan Joslyn had carried across half a continent. In a sandbar not far away was a fresh excavation, and just beyond Joslyn's outstretched hand lay a buckskin bag, half full of a substance that gleamed dull yellow as Captain Bradley poured it out in his hand.

He stood for a long while staring down at the nuggets in his palm. George Joslyn had made his strike at last.

There was no doubt of that. Gold. Nugget gold. That meant that somewhere nearby lay a vein capable of enriching many men. Capable of turning a nation's eyes west.

A coyote on the crest of the hill lifted his lonely cry into empty space; after a while an answering wail floated back through the gathering twilight. Slowly Captain Bradley tilted his hand and let the gold spill out. He up-ended the buckskin sack and threw it into the water. Stooping, he picked up gold pan, shovel and miner's pick and tossed them far out into the forest. Then without a glance at the dead man, he limped slowly downstream. Once he paused, thinking he had heard a small movement in the hillside above him; he listened for a moment, and then, hearing nothing, gave a brief laugh and walked on.

Full darkness had fallen by the time he reached camp. "Find Joslyn?" Conners asked.

"Joslyn," the captain said, "has deserted."

He went to his tent, lit a candle and sat down to finish the letter to his wife. He had been writing for only a few minutes when he was aware of a quiet step outside. He looked up to see the tall figure of Chief Qualchee standing in the entryway of the tent.

"I am here," the Indian said.

He held a blanket wrapped around him against the growing chill of night. Captain Bradley gazed silently at him for a while, then he said, "You will lead us to the pass?"

Perhaps it was the captain's imagination again, but he thought a brief glint illumined the dark eyes, a wordless communication that pierced all barriers of race and color and showed him the soul of Qualchee. The Indian said softly, "Would Qualchee speak with a forked tongue and let the straight words of the white man shame him?"

Then he was gone and the entryway lay black and empty. The captain stared at the spot where the Indian had stood. There on the dusty ground lay a hunting arrow. The captain picked it up. The head was sharp and barbed. The feathers bound to the notched end were red, green and white.

Captain Bradley shivered and gingerly laid the arrow on the improvised desk across his knees. He picked up his pen, chewed thoughtfully at its end for a moment and then, the faintest ghost of a smile touching his lips, started writing.

. . . Qualchee came, as he promised he would. He says he will lead us to the pass tomorrow. Somehow I have confidence that he will. He impresses me as a man of honor. . . .

THE FRAUDULENT SKUNK

By A. B. GUTHRIE, JR.

A. B. Guthrie, Jr., author of THE BIG SKY and THE WAY
WEST, generally considered to be among the best Western
novels of our time, shows himself to be equally adept at
the short story form with the light and rib-tickling item
which follows. This one is the story of the time Shorty,
the sheepherder, got into a saloon, locked himself in, and
proceeded to drink the place dry, much to the horror of
the other thirsty citizens.

THERE were five men in the back room of the Moon
Dance bar—three ranchers, a hay hand and a cattle buyer
—all idled by the rain that was beating outside. They had
quit their pinochle game, the cards and chips lying forgotten on the green table, and were listening to old Ray
Gibler who'd started on one of his stories.

Then Ray saw me and grinned and held out his big
hand. "How, Tenderfoot."

"I'll listen," I said to Ray. I took off my slicker.

"I was just talking. Ought to be making tracks."

One of the ranchers said, "You ain't gonna ride herd on
no dudes today."

"My woman's probably on the hunt for me."

"I'll buy a drink," I said.

Ray gave me his wide grin again. It made deep wrinkles
in his leathery cheeks. "I don't like to get in the habit of
refusin'."

I yelled to the bartender for a round. "What was this
about a skunk?"

"Well, I'll tell you—"

Ray doodled the ice in his ditchwater highball with one horny finger. . . .

It was Shorty, the sheepherder, had the skunk, and it happened right here, right in this bar, and there was rooms overhead just like now, only you boys wouldn't remember it, being still slick-eared.

Shorty was new to the town then, but it didn't take us long to find he was all sheepherder. Had a fine, steady thirst and a free hand with money. He had been herding for George I. Smith for five-six months when he decided he couldn't stand thirst nor prosperity any longer. He came to town, a sawed-off, humpy feller with a mop of black hair and a habit of talking to himself, like all herders.

He got fired up good the first day and kep' the blaze going maybe a week, while his whiskers stooled out and his clothes got dirtier and dirtier, and a man meeting him was careful to get on the wind side.

He slept all one day under the hitch rack in back of the Moon Dance Mercantile Company, and when he woke up that night he was just as dry as he was broke, which is as dry as a man can get. He tried moochin' drinks, going from one place to another, but he'd run out of credit, too, and all he got was a bad eye and good advice from the men who had his money.

I was right here, on business you might say, that night when Shorty came in and asked if the roof didn't never leak.

Whitey Hanson said, polishing a glass, "It's leaked

plenty. I set 'em up for you three or four times. Git out!"

Shorty tried to argue. "My money, you got it."

"Ah-h. Why'n't you git back on the job?"

There was a couple of curly wolves in the bar, along with Whitey and Shorty and me. Anyhow, they figured they was curly. One of them was Rough Red Rourke and the other Stub Behr. Seeing Shorty, they moseyed over. "*Ba-a-a*," Red said in his ear, loud enough to bust an eardrum.

"Way round 'em!" Stub yelled.

Red grabbed Shorty by the shoulder. "Them pore ewes are missin' you, sweetheart."

Together they ran Shorty limp-legged through the door and pitched him in the street. Shorty got up slow, talking to himself, and dragged off.

Whitey Hanson thought that was good stuff. He said thankee to Red and Stub and poured drinks on the house.

Must have been a couple of hours later—anyhow along towards midnight—when Shorty showed up again, and not alone neither. He had a skunk with him, carrying it along by the tail so it couldn't do business. Old-timers have seen that trick worked many a time in days before saloons got to be hideyholes for spooners. Of course we didn't know the skunk was Shorty's pet.

Red saw him first and a big, drunk smile came on his face. He couldn't see the skunk on account of Shorty was carrying it on the off side. "Hey, Stub," he said, "look what I see." Then he hollered, "*Ba-a-a-a!*" at Shorty, so loud the roof shook.

He made for Shorty, and Shorty saw him and a look

came on his face. He swung the skunk around. "By damn!" he said.

Red stopped like he'd been butted by a bull. Stub was trying to slip out of sight.

"Way round 'em!" Shorty said, and pointed the skunk and held it low, so's its front feet almost touched the floor. "Git out, both you! Git!"

He hazed them around towards the door, still holding the skunk low, business end to. It takes an awful brave man to face up to a skunk. Red and Stub wasn't that curly. They got.

Shorty closed the door after them and headed for the bar like a trout for a hopper. This was the business he had come for. He held the skunk up. To Whitey he said, "Set 'em up or I set 'im down!"

"Sure, Shorty, sure. Don't set 'im down. Nice work. Shorty." Whitey came from behind the bar and stretched his arm away out and shook Shorty's loose fist. "Them fellers couldn't buffalo you, Shorty."

Some of the rest of us ambled up, not too close, and told Shorty he sure did shine. Shorty said, "Wasn't nuthin'. Wasn't nuthin'."

"It sure was, Shorty. Sure was."

I reckon all that glory was too much for Shorty. He wasn't used to compliments, but just to hearing sheep bleat and bartenders say hell no, they wouldn't trust him for a drink and why didn't he go to work. Yep, it must have been too much for him. Anyhow, he dropped the skunk.

Whitey jumped the counter like an antelope and tore out the back. Tubby Adams got squoze so hard in the doorway he swore his pants wouldn't fit for a month, being way big in the waist and way short in the leg. It must have taken us all of five seconds to clear out, leaving Shorty and his skunk in the saloon—with the whisky.

Well, we got together outside, still breathing hard, and held a rump session by the front door. Whitey was there, of course, and me and two or three cow hands and the printer for the Messenger, who was celebrating on account of getting the paper out just one day late. We couldn't see inside; Whitey always kept the shades drawn and the place dim-lit.

"Boys," Whitey said, hearing a cork pop, "we got to get him out of there."

One of the cow hands—Pete his name was, Pete Gleeson —said, "I could open the door just a crack and shoot the skunk if I had sump'n to shoot him with."

"I can't have the place stunk up," Whitey said quick. "I gotta think about my customers. I gotta think about the hotel. Ain't anyone wants to drink or sleep in a stunk-up place." He gave us an anxious look.

"I couldn't guarantee to shoot him dead first crack," the cow-poke said.

"I figure the place is already stunk up," I told Whitey.

He put his nose to the keyhole. "Maybe not. I can't smell nothin' yet. Maybe that skunk's used to Shorty." He raised his voice. "If you don't come out, Shorty, I'll have to get the law." He waited for an answer. "I'll get the sheriff."

From inside we heard Shorty holler, " 'Way round 'em, Shep."

"That settles it. I will get the sheriff," Whitey said. "You fellers stand guard." He moved off down the street, making for the jail.

After a while he came back, bringing Sheriff McKenzie with him. I had an idea he had been chewing McKenzie's ear off on the way.

"All right, Sheriff," Whitey said when they came up to us.

McKenzie gnawed on his mustache. "Now, Whitey, let's augur on this. What you want me to do, anyway?"

"Get Shorty and the skunk outta my place of business, that's what," Whitey told him. "And no stink!"

"It's a big order, Whitey, a mighty big order," the sheriff said.

Whitey never did like the sheriff much. "The taxes I pay, looks like you would have an idea."

"Your paying taxes don't seem to help me much right now."

"You got a reputation as a fast man with a gun. Anyhow, you used to have. But watch you don't hit my new mirror."

McKenzie chewed his whiskers some more. "I don't know. I wouldn't say I was *that* fast."

Tubby Adams said, "Try persuadin'. Looks like Shorty would feel plumb agreeable by now."

The sheriff walked up to the door. "This here's the law,

Shorty. This here's the sheriff. You gotta come outta there, Shorty. Best come peaceful. Best not make a stink."

What he got back was a song, or a piece of it. It sounded real pretty there in the dark.

> *"He's a killer and a hater!*
> *He's the great annihilator!*
> *He's a terror of the boundless prairie."*

"Don't look like I'm doin' any good," McKenzie said, turning around to us. He tried it again. "I don't want no trouble, Shorty. You gonna make me come in and git you?"

This time Shorty answered, "Yah."

The sheriff backed away. "This is serious, sure enough." He kept bitin' his whiskers and got an idea. "We'll just throw open the door and let the skunk come out by hisself."

We all looked at each other. It wasn't for nothin' we had put McKenzie in the sheriff's office, you bet. McKenzie put his hand on the knob while the rest of us got ready to light out. Only the knob wouldn't turn. Shorty wasn't as dumb as you might think.

"You get any smell?" Whitey asked.

McKenzie put his snoot to the keyhole. "Yep."

"Oh, hell!"

"Rotgut," the sheriff said. "The stink of plain rotgut. Nothin' else. Reckon that skunk's ashamed of his equipment by comparison."

Tubby hitched his pants. "Long as you won't let anybody shoot that woods pussy, ain't nothin' to do but starve Shorty out."

"Starve 'im out!" Whitey bawled. "Starve him out, you damn' fool! You think he'll want to eat?"

"I hadn't give proper thought to that," Tubby answered.

The printer swallowed another hiccup. "Have to wait till the well runs dry."

Whitey clapped his hands to his head.

"I could use a drink myself," the sheriff put in.

Come to think of it, all of us could. From here on we began to think deep.

I called the boys away from the door so's Shorty couldn't hear. "Ain't there a way to poison skunks? What they eat, anyhow?"

"Chickens," Tubby answered. "Damn 'em!"

"I hear tell they eat frogs and snakes," the printer said.

While we were thinking frogs and snakes, Shorty began on another tune.

> *"Drink that rotgut, drink that rotgut,*
> *Drink that redeye, boys;*
> *It don't make a damn wherever we land,*
> *We hit her up for joy."*

"A frog now," Tubby said while he scratched his head with one hand. "Or snakes. Then there's the poison."

"I guess it ain't no trouble for you to put your hand on a frog or a snake any old time," Whitey said.

"My boy's got himself a collection. I don't figger he'd

72

mind partin' with a frog or a snake." Tubby licked his mouth. "Not in a good cause, anyway."

"It might work," the printer said. "Worth tryin'."

So Tubby said he'd get a frog, and Pete Gleeson— that was the cow hand—said he'd rout the druggist out and get some strychnine.

By and by they came back, Tubby holding a little old frog that was still mostly tadpole and Pete bringing powdered strychnine in a paper bag.

"First," said Sheriff McKenzie, taking charge of things, "we got to poison the frog. Pry his mouth open, one of you."

We gave the frog a good pinch of poison, with a drop of water for a chaser, and nosed him up to the crack and tried to goose him in. No go. That frog wouldn't budge.

After a while we found out it was because he was dead already.

"The frog idea ain't so good," the sheriff said. "Even with a live frog, it wouldn't work. A frog moves by hoppin'. How's he gonna hop *under* a door? Just bump his head, is all. Sumpn quick and slithery would be the ticket, like a snake."

"And don't poison him inside," I said. "Poison him out."

" 'Nother thing," Pete Gleeson put in. "Roll 'im in something sticky first, like flypaper."

You can see we was all thinkin' dry and hard.

Tubby went back to the house and got a garter snake, and Pete waked the druggist up again to get a sheet of flypaper. The druggist came along with him this time, figuring it wasn't any use to try to sleep.

Tubby and the sheriff didn't mind handlin' the snake.

The strychnine clung fine to the flypaper stickem, and the stickem clung fine to the snake. You never saw a snake like that one! All powdered up pretty, with a kind of a flounce around the neck where the strychnine was extra thick. You would have thought it was going to a wedding.

It could still crawl, though. Tubby pointed it at the crack and let go, and it slipped inside slick as butter.

Shorty was singing "Red Wing" now, only you could tell he had already sung his best and didn't have much class left in him.

"How long," asked Whitey, "does it take strychnine to work?"

The druggist chewed the question over with himself and came out with, "Depends."

"We'll give 'er plenty of time," Whitey said. "I won't open the place till mornin'."

"We done a lot of thinkin' for you," Tubby said, looking at Whitey sad-eyed. "Got a frog, too, and a snake."

"All right. All right, I'll set 'em up in the morning." Whitey talked as if it hurt him.

So we all dragged away, figuring, of course, to be on deck come opening time, which we were.

Whitey had the sheriff with him again, and there was all the rest of us, plus quite a crowd who'd heard about the doings.

"Might have to break the door down," Whitey said. "I can't unlock her if she's locked from inside." He turned to McKenzie, "Sheriff, do your duty."

The sheriff waited a while, as if to show he wasn't taking

orders from the likes of Whitey. Then he up and turns the knob and the door swung open.

It was just like we'd left it, the place was, except for a couple of empty bottles. No Shorty. No skunk. No snake. No nothing. It was just like we'd left it, except Whitey's new mirror was busted all to hell, which made us feel awful sorry for him. Business took up as usual.

Ray drained his glass. "I was tellin' the boys before you came in it was a stinkless skunk. Been separated from his ammunition, you might say, though we didn't know it, of course. The place didn't smell a bit worse than it does now."

"You mean the skunk ate the snake and went off and died, and so Shorty left?" I asked.

"Oh, no. That wasn't the way of it at all. What happened was we cured Shorty. He had picked up his skunk and lit out. Never touched a drop afterwards. He said he'd seen snakes plenty of times while drinkin', but by grab when he saw one with frostin' on it, it was time to quit."

LONESOME RIDE

By ERNEST HAYCOX

LONESOME RIDE is the tense, suspenseful story of three prospectors who learn they're about to be robbed of their gold, and of one of them who volunteers to take the lonesome and dangerous ride to get the gold safely put away. It's a couple of days' ride that's necessary, with the chance that killers are waiting with drawn guns at any lonely spot along the way.

Ernest Haycox, probably America's most popular Western writer, and on whose stories STAGECOACH, UNION PACIFIC, and other movies have been based, died suddenly not long ago. He'll be forever missed by friends and readers.

JOHNNY POTTER had only squatted himself in the cabin's doorway for a smoke when he heard Plez Neal's footsteps rattling along the stony trail in a rapid return from town. Plez came across the sooty shadows of the yard and made a mysterious motion at Johnny. He said, "Come inside."

Johnny followed Plez into the cabin and closed the door. A third partner, Thad Jessup, lay on a bunk, stripped to socks, trousers and iron-stained undershirt. He had been half asleep but his eyes opened and were instantly alert.

"Buck Miller's in town again," said Plez Neal. "He's huddled up with that saddle-faced barkeep in the Blue Bucket. They were talking about me—I could tell." He went over to a soapbox to fill his pipe from a red tobacco can.

"Add those three other fellows that drifted in yester-day," said Thad. "There's your crowd. They smell honey."

"They smell us," said Plez. "Now we're sittin' ducks, not knowin' which way we'll be flushed."

"How'd you suppose they know we're worth a hold-up?" asked Thad.

"Talk of the camp. I wish we hadn't let that damned dust pile up so long."

Johnny Potter sat hunched over on the edge of a box, arms across his knees. He spread out his fingers and stared at them while he listened to the talk of his partners. Both Plez and Thad were middle-aged men from the Willamette who had left their families behind them to come here and grub out gold enough to go back and buy valley farms. He was the youngster who had a good many more years to throw away than they had; he didn't dread the loss of the dust as they did, but he understood how they felt about it. He riffled his fingers through the ragged, curling edges of his hair and once he looked toward the fireplace, beneath whose stones lay $20,000 in lard cans. His eyes were flashing blue against the mahogany burn of his skin; he was one of those slender young men whose face had a listening silence on it. In the little crevices around his features boyishness and rough knowledge lay uneasily together.

"We've made our stake," said Thad. "We could pack and pull out."

"Won't do. We've got some protection in camp. On the trail we'd be easy marks."

77

"But," said Thad, "if we stay here we'll get knocked over. It's a Mexican standoff. If they want us they'll get us. Just a question of how and when."

There was a silence, during which time Johnny Potter decided his partners had no answer to the problem. He straightened on the box and made a small flat gesture with both hands against his legs. "The three of us would travel too slow, but one of us could travel light and fast. I'll take my horse, and your horse, Plez. Tonight. With a head start I can outrun that crowd and get into The Dalles with the dust in four days."

"Why two horses?" asked Plez.

Johnny nodded toward the fireplace. "That stuff weighs around a hundred pounds. I'll change horses as I go."

Plez said, "We'll cook up some bacon and you can take bread. You can make cold camps."

"I got to have coffee," said Johnny. "Pack the dust in the two sets of saddlebags."

Thad said, "If they're watchin' us, they'll notice you're gone in the morning."

"While you're packing," said Johnny, "I'll drop in at the Blue Bucket and play sick. Tomorrow you tack a smallpox sign on the cabin. They'll think I'm in bed."

Plez thought about it, sucking at his pipe. "Johnny, it's two hundred miles to The Dalles. If they pick up your tracks you're a gone chicken."

"Fall of the dice," said Johnny and opened the door and stepped into a full mountain darkness. Cabin lights and campfires glimmered through the trees and along the gulch below him, and men's voices drifted in the windless air.

He took the trail to the creek bottom, threaded his way past tents and gravel piles thrown back from bedrock, and came upon Canyon City's shanties wedged at the bottom of the ravine. The sound of the saloons reached out to him. He turned into the Blue Bucket, stumbling slightly; he saw a few friends at the poker tables and nodded to them in a drawn and gloomy manner, and he made a place for himself at the bar beside Pete Hewitt. The saddle-faced barkeep was at the far end of the counter, talking to a man whose face Johnny couldn't see at the moment. The barkeep broke off the talk long enough to bring Johnny a bottle and glass, and went back to his talk. Johnny took his cheer straight and poured another. The barkeep was at the edge of his vision; he noted the man's eyes roll toward him.

Pete Hewitt said, "What the hell's the matter with you, Johnny?"

"I ache, I'm hot, I'm cold, I feel terrible."

"Ague. Get good and drunk."

Johnny eased his weight on the footrail, swinging enough to have a look at the man with the barkeep. It was Buck Miller, no question—big nose, face the color of an old gray boulder, a set of rough and raking eyes. Johnny called the barkeep back to pay for his drinks. He said to Hewitt, "I'm goin' to bed and I'm not getting up for a week."

Leaving the saloon, he remembered a chore and dropped into the Mercantile to buy caps for his revolver; when he came from the store he noticed Buck Miller in the door-way of the Blue Bucket, staring directly at him. Short gusts of sensation wavered up and down the back of John-ny's neck, as he traveled the stony gulch back to the cabin. "No question about it," he thought. "He's got his mind made up for that dust."

Plez met him in the yard's darkness and murmured rest-lessly, "Come on." He followed Plez along the creek to a corral which boxed in a bit of the hillside and found the horses packed to go. He tried his cinches and patted the saddlebags. There were two sets of bags, one behind his saddle and one hooked to a light rig thrown over the spare horse. Plez said, "Bacon and bread's in your blanket roll. Coffee too—but get along without it, Johnny. A fire means trouble."

"Got to have coffee, trouble or no trouble."

"Tobacco and matches there. It's Thad's rifle in the boot. Shoots better than yours."

Johnny Potter stepped to his saddle, taking hold of the lead rope. Thad whispered, "Listen," and the three of them were stone-still, dredging the night with their senses. A few stray sounds drifted up the slope; a shape passed across the beam of a campfire. "Somebody around the cabin," whispered Thad. "Get out of here, Johnny."

Plez said in his kind and troubled voice: "Don't hold no foolish notions. If you get in a vise, dump the damned dust and run."

Johnny turned up the ravine, reached the first bench of the hill, and paralleled the gulch as it ran northward toward the wider meadows of the John Day, two miles distant. He was tight with the first strain of this affair; he listened for the sound of a gun behind him, he made quick search of himself for things done right or done wrong, and presently he fell down the hill into the John Day and saw the dull glittering of the creek's ford ahead of him.

He held back a moment. There were lights along the valley, from other diggings and other cabins, and the trail was well traveled by men going to and coming from Canyon City. At this moment he neither saw nor heard anybody and left the shadows of the hill and soon crossed the creek. The racket of his horses in the water was a signal soon answered, for, looking behind him, Johnny saw a shape slide out of the canyon shadows and come to the ford. Johnny swung from the trail at once and put himself into the willows beside the river.

He waited, hearing the rider cross the water and pass down the trail perhaps two hundred feet and there stop and remain motionless for a full three minutes. Suddenly Johnny understood he had made a mistake; he had tipped his hand when he had gone into the store to buy the caps. It wasn't a thing a sick man would do.

The rider wheeled and walked his horse toward the ford. His shadow came abreast Johnny and faded but at the creek he swung again and came back, clearly hunting and clearly dissatisfied. It was time, Johnny guessed, to use a little pressure; drawing his gun, he cocked the hammer and sent that lean dry little sound into the night. The rider whipped about, immediately racing over the ford and running full tilt toward Canyon City. He would be going back for the rest of Miller's bunch.

Johnny came out of the brush and went down the trail at a hard run, passing cabins and campfires and sometimes hearing men hail him. He followed the windings of this roughbeaten highway as it matched the windings of the river; he watched the shadows before him; he listened for the rumor of running horses behind him and once—the better to catch the tom-toms of pursuit—he stopped to give the horses a blow and to check the saddlebags. The lights of the diggings at last faded, and near midnight he reached another cluster of cabins, all dark and sleeping, and turned from the valley into the hills. Before him lay something less than two hundred miles of country, timber, rough mountain creases, open grass plains and rivers lying deep in straight-walled canyons.

He slowed the horses to a walk and wound through the black alleys of these hills while the night wore on and the silence deepened; in the first paling dawn he stopped at a creek for a drink and a smoke and went on steadily thereafter until noon found him on the edge of a timber overlooking a meadowed corridor through these hills. Out there lay the main trail which he watched for a few minutes; then he staked the horses, cooked his coffee and curled on the needlespongy soil to rest.

It was less than real sleep. He heard the horses moving, he came wide awake at the staccato echoes of a woodpecker, and drifted away again, and moved back and forth across the border of consciousness, straining into the silence, mistrusting the silence. He woke before sunset, tired. He threw on the gear and moved the horses to the creek and let them browse in the bottom grasses while he boiled up another pot of coffee. Afterwards he returned to the edge of the timber and, as long as light lasted, he watched the trail which was a wriggling pale line across the tawny meadows below. He had to take that trail for the speed it offered him, but when he took it he also exposed himself. Thus far he had been pretty secure in the breadth of the country behind him—a pinpoint lost within a thousand square miles of hills and crisscross gullies. Ahead of him, though, the trail squeezed itself narrowly through a bottleneck of very rough land. Buck Miller knew about that—and might be waiting there.

Under darkness he moved over the flats to the trail and ran its miles down. He stopped to water at a creek and later, well beyond the creek, he paused to listen and thought he heard the scudding of other horses, though the sounds were so abraded by distance that he could not locate them. Riding west, he saw the ragged rising of hills through the silver gloom; the trail went downgrade, struck the graveled bottom of a dry wash, and fell gradually into a pocket at the base of the hills. His horse, seeing some odd thing, whipped aside, going entirely off the trail. A moment later it plunged both forefeet into a washout, dropped to its knees and flung Johnny Potter from the saddle.

He turned in the air, he struck, he felt pain slice him through; the odor of blood was in his nostrils and his senses ran out like the fast tide, leaving him dumb on the ground. Then the pain accumulated into one rolling shock wave and revived him with its acute misery. He turned and he sat up, moving fast to confirm or throw aside his fears. His left leg burned from hip to ankle and he kicked it out straight with a rough wish to know the worst. Nothing

83

wrong there. He tried his right leg, he moved his arms, he stood up. He was all right.

He couldn't get rid of his haste. All through the preceding night a loneliness had worked its way with him and had made him feel that every shadow concealed trouble; the same loneliness now gave him the notion that listening ears were everywhere around him and that men were rushing toward him. He crouched in the washout and ran his hands along the down horse's front legs and discovered the break. He wanted a smoke, risk or no risk, and he filled his pipe and lighted it close to the ground. Then he brought in the lead horse—which had strayed out toward grass—transferred the gear to it from the down horse. When he was ready to travel again he put a bullet into the head of the down horse, the report shouting and rumbling and rocketing away in all directions, filling the world with a tremendous racket, and traveling on and never seeming to end. It appeared to follow him and point him out when he rode forward.

The trail fell into a black pocket, reached a creek, and swung with the creek around a long bend, bringing the North Star from Johnny's right shoulder point to a spot in the sky directly before him. In the first streaky moments of dawn he found himself in the bottom grasses and the willow clumps of Bridge Creek near its junction with the John Day. The ridges rose to either side of him and he sat a moment motionless in the saddle and felt naked under such exposure; it would be a better thing to get out of this meadow land and to lose himself in the rough and treeless stringers of earth which made a hundred hidden pockets as they marched higher and higher over the mountains toward central Oregon. But that was the slow way, and he had not enough knowledge of the country to leave the trail and thus, his restless nerves pricking him into action, he went down the creek bottom at the best gallop he could kick out of his horse and reached the still more open bottoms of the John Day.

He hunched his shoulders, listening for a shot and expecting it. He pushed his horse along and tried not to realize that he was asking too much of it. A fine sweat broke over his face like an itch and he reached deep for wind. It was a wonderful thing to at last see the trail rise up from the river through a notch and go directly into the broken land. As soon as the ridge permitted him, he went up its side and got into another draw; he pressed on, climbing and turning and searching the land until he felt his horse lag. Thereupon he changed his course until he reached a ridge from which he saw the trail visible in the ravine below. He fed the horse and put it on picket in a gulley and lay down to rest.

Through his curtain of sleep, broken as it was by strain and weariness, he heard the clear running sound of horses below. He reached for his rifle, rolled and crawled to the rim of the ridge all in a motion, and saw four men swinging along the trail below him; the lead man's head was bent, carefully reading signs, and in a moment this man signaled for a halt and swung his horse around, bringing his face into view—that dark skin and big boney nose sharp in the sunlight. The four made a close group on the trail while they talked. Their words lifted toward Johnny:

"No," said Buck Miller, "we've gone too far this way. The kid left the trail back there where the ridge began. He went the other side. We'll go back and pick up his tracks."

"He's tryin' to fool us," said another man. "He may be settin' behind a rock waitin' for us to walk right into his shot."

"He's just a kid," said Buck Miller. "He'll run—he won't stand and fight. All he wants to do is keep ahead of us and get to The Dalles."

The other man wasn't convinced. He said, "You go back and pick up his tracks while I ride this way a couple miles. If I don't see anything I'll cut over the ridge and find you."

"No," said Buck Miller. "If I see anything moving ahead of me I'll shoot it—and it might turn out to be you. We'll stick together. When we locate the kid we can box him in. He ain't far ahead. He's got two horses and the dust weighs enough to slow him down."

The other man said, "He's got the advantage and I don't like it much. He can watch us come and he's above us."

Miller shook his head. "If it was a hard customer we were trailin', I'd say you were right. But he's never shot a man. That makes a difference, Jeff. It's a hard thing to pull the trigger if you ain't done it before—and while he's makin' up his mind about it, we'll get around him. I figure we can bring him to a stop. Then one of us can slip behind and get above him. I can hit him the first bullet, anywhere up to four hundred yards."

Johnny Potter drew his rifle forward and laid its stock

against his cheek. He had Buck Miller framed in the sights, with no doubt left in his mind; it was a matter of kill or be killed—it was that plain. Yet he was astonished that Buck Miller knew him so well; for he had trouble making his finger squeeze the slack from the trigger. It was a hard thing to kill—and that was something he hadn't known. "Well," he thought, "I've got to do it," and had persuaded himself to fire when the group whirled and ran back along the trail. He had missed his chance.

It would take them a couple hours, he guessed. He sat still, sweating and uncomfortable, watching them disappear around the rough bends of the ravine; he swung his head back and forth to clear it and he rose reluctantly and went to the horse, pulling up the picket. With Miller behind him, he had a chance for a clear run on the trail, and maybe he could set a trap. He figured it out in his mind as he rode directly down the ridge's side into the trail and galloped westward. They were careless in the way they boomed along; they had no particular fear of him—which made the trap possible, maybe.

He came to a creek and turned the horse into it; he dismounted and dropped belly flat in the water at the feet of the horse, and he drank in great strangling, greedy gusts, rooting his face and head through the water like a hog snouting up acorns from the earth. He had to pull himself away from that luxurious coolness and felt the coolness go away as he traveled on. The canyon began to grow both narrow and crooked, and the hills rose more steeply around him. Somewhere ahead of him the canyon would run out and the trail would then move directly up the face of the hills. When he took that he was an open target. Meanwhile the creek, coming closer to its source, fed a thicker and thicker stand of willows and presently he left the trail and he put the horse well back into the willows. He walked a few yards away from the horse, parted the willows and made himself a covert. He took a few trial sights with the rifle down the trail, and sat back to wait. He closed his eyes, gently groaning. Canyon City was maybe a hundred miles behind him and The Dalles a like distance ahead.

It was well into the afternoon when he heard the small vibrations of their coming. He turned on his stomach and brought the gun through the willows, took another trial sight, and had the muzzle against the bend when they came around it, riding single file and riding carelessly. They had convinced themselves he wouldn't stop to fight. They came on loosely scattered, the lead man watching the trail and Buck Miller bringing up the rear.

Miller was the man he wanted and he had terrible moments of indecision, swinging and lifting the gun to bring it on Miller; but the other three made a screen for Miller and at last Johnny took a sure aim on the lead man, now fifty feet away, and killed him with a shot through the chest.

He dropped the rifle and brought up his revolver as he watched the lead man fall and the riderless horse charge directly up the trail. The other three wheeled and ran for the shelter of the bend. Two of them made it, but Johnny's snap shot caught the third man's horse, and it dropped and threw its rider into the gravel. The man cried as he struck and his arm swung behind him in an unnatural way;

he got to his knees and turned his face—bleeding and staring and shocked—toward Johnny. He tried to get to his
feet, he shouted, he fell on his chest and began to crawl
for the bend on one arm.

Johnny retreated into the willows, got his horse and
came into the trail at a charging run. The fallen man made
no move; the other two were sheltered behind the point
of the ravine. Rushing along the trail, away from them,
Johnny overtook the riderless horse, seized its reins as he
passed by, and towed it on. He was, presently, around
another turn of the trail and thus for a moment well sheltered; but in the course of a half mile the trail reached a
dead end, with the bald rough hills rising in a long hard
slant; and up this stiff-tilted way the trail climbed by one
short switchback upon another. He took to the switch-
backs, coming immediately out of the canyon. Within five
minutes he was exposed to them against the hillside, and
waited for a long-reaching rifle bullet to strike. He looked
into the canyon, not yet seeing them. He shoved his horse
on with a steady heel gouging. He rode tense, the sharp
cold sensations rippling through him; he jumped when
the first shot broke the windless, heated air. The bullet,
falling short, made its small "thut" in the ground below
him. He kept climbing, exposed and at their mercy, and
having no shelter anywhere. He heard the second shot
strike, still short, and he turned and, from his increased
elevation, he saw the two crouched behind the point of
land. They were reloading. The third man was still motionless on the trail.

He kept climbing, his horse grinding wind heavily in

and out. He tried a chance shot with his revolver and watched both men jump aside though he knew the bullet came nowhere near. They were both aiming, and they fired together. It was the foreshortened distance of the hillside which deceived them and left their bullets below him again. By that time he had reached a short bench and ran across it, temporarily out of their sight; then the hill began again and the trail once more began its climbing turns, exposing him. At this higher level he was beyond decent shooting and he noted that the two had abandoned their rifles and were bending over the man lying on the trail. He stared at the crests above him, some of the tension going out of him, and he let the horse drop to a slightly slower gait. An hour later he reached the top of the hill and faced a broken country before him; bald sagebrush slopes folded one into another and rocky ravines searched through them.

He dismounted and gave the horses a rest while he sat down on the edge of the hill and kept watch on the two dark shapes now far below. They hadn't come on. From his position he now had them on his hip unless they back-tracked through this slashed-up country and took another ridge to ride around him. As long as he stood here they couldn't climb the open slope. He stretched out, sup-porting his head with a hand. His throat was so dry that the flesh seemed brittle and he breathed with tremendous effort and couldn't get enough air. The memory of the cold creek recently tasted became a distant memory, an aggravation; he closed his lids and felt gritty particles scraping across his eyeballs—and suddenly he felt a sharp

stinging on his cheek and jumped to his feet. He put a
hand to his cheek and drew a short bit of sagebrush from
his skin. He had fallen asleep and had rolled against the
sagebrush.

The two men were at the creek, resting in the shade of
the willows—no doubt waiting night. He rose to the saddle of the borrowed horse and started along the ravine
which curled around a bald butte. Near sundown the
ravine came out to the breakoff of this string of hills and
he saw the slope roll far down into a basin about a mile
wide, on the far side of which lay a dark rim. Beyond the
rim the high desert ran away to the west and the north;
through the haze, off to the west, he saw the vaguest sil-
houette of snow peaks in the Cascades. He descended the
slope as sunset came on in flame and violence.

Darkness found him beside a seepage of water in a
pocket of the high rolling sagebrush land. He fed the
horses half the remaining oats, ate his bacon and bread
and built a fire to cook his coffee. He killed the fire and
made himself a little spell of comfort with his pipe. Haze
covered the sky, creating a solid blackness; the horses
stirred around the scanty grasses. He rose and retreated
twenty yards from where his fire had been and sat against
a juniper. He got to thinking of the two men; they knew
he was somewhere in this area—and they no doubt guessed
he'd camp near water. If he were in their boots, he decided,
he wouldn't try to find a man in this lonesomeness of rolling earth; he'd lay out on some ridge and wait for the man
to come into view. The trail—the main trail to The Dalles
—was a couple miles west of him.

He seemed to be strangling in water; he flung out a hand, striking his knuckles on the coarse-pebbled soil, and then he sprang up and rammed his head against the juniper. He had been sleeping again. He walked to the seepage and flattened on his stomach, alternately drinking and dousing his head until coldness cleared his mind; then he led the horses to water and let them fill, and resumed his ride, following little creases he could scarcely see, toward a shallow summit. An hour later he came upon the main trail and turned north with it.

The country rose to long swells and fell into barren hollows which he marked more by the feel of the trail than by any decent view; nothing broke the shadows except an occasional upthrust of rock ledge. Having been once over this route he knew the deep canyon of the Deschutes was in front of him, with a wooden toll bridge, but of its exact distance from his present location he had no idea. Around midnight he identified the blurred outline of a house ahead of him—a single wayside station sitting out in the emptiness—and he left the trail to circle the station at a good distance. By daylight he found himself in a rutty little defile passing up through a flinty ridge and here, at a summit strewn with fractured rocks, he camped his horses in a pit and crawled back to the edge of the trail, making himself a trench in the loose rubble. The defile was visible all the way to its foot; the plain beyond was in full view. Two riders were coming on across the plain toward the ridge.

He settled his gun on the rocks and, while he waited, he slowly squirmed his body against the flinty soil, like an animal gathering tension for a leap. They were still beyond his reach when they came to the foot of the defile and stopped; and then, in tremendous disappointment, he saw that they would not walk into the same trap twice. They talked a moment, with Buck Miller making his gestures around the ridge. Afterwards Miller left the trail and traveled eastward along the foot of the ridge, away from Johnny, for a half mile or so before he turned into the slope and began to climb. The other man also left the trail, passing along the foot of the ridge below Johnny.

Johnny crawled back into the rocks and scrambled in and out of the rough pits and boulder chunks, paralleling the man below him. He went a quarter mile before he flattened and put his head over the rim, and saw the rider angling upward. Johnny retreated and ran another short distance, gauging where he'd meet the man head-on, and returned to the rim. He squeezed himself between two rocks, with the aperture giving him a view of the rider so slowly winding his way forward. He looked to his left to keep Buck Miller in sight and saw Miller slanting still farther away as he climbed. He returned his attention to the man below him and pulled his rifle into position; he watched the man grow wider and taller as he got nearer; he saw the man's eyes sweep the rim. Suddenly, with a fair shot open to him, Johnny stood up from the rocks— not knowing why he gave the man that much grace—and aimed on a shape suddenly in violent motion. The man discovered him and tried to turn the horse as he drew. Johnny's bullet tore its hole through the man's chest, from side to side.

The pitching horse threw the man from the saddle and plunged away. Johnny gave him no more thought, immediately running back toward his own horses. Miller, having reached the crest of the ridge half a mile distant, paused a moment there to hear the shot, to orient it—and to see Johnny. Then Miller ran down the slope, toward the toll bridge, toward The Dalles. Johnny reached his animals and filled his pipe and smoked it while he watched Miller fade out of sight in the swells of land to the north. Now he had trouble in front of him instead of behind him—for there was no other way to reach The Dalles except by the toll bridge. But the odds were better—it was one and one now. When he had finished his pipe he started forward, plodding a dusty five miles an hour along a downhill land under a sky filling with sunlight. The trail reached a breakoff, with the river running through a lava gorge far below. He took the narrow trail, winding from point to point.

Rounding a last bend and dropping down a last bench, he found the bridge before him— a row of planks nailed on two logs thrown over waters boiling violently between narrow walls. There was a pack string on the far side and four men sitting in the dust. Coming to the bridge he had a look at the men over the way, and the shed beyond the house, and the crooked grade reaching up the hill behind the bridge. He went across and met the tollkeeper as the latter came out of the house.

"Two dollars," said the tollkeeper.

"Can you fill that nose bag with oats?"

"All right."

Johnny Potter pushed the horses on to a trough and let them drink. He waited for the man to furnish the oats and went to a water barrel with a cup hanging to it. He drank five cups of water straight down. When the man brought the oats Johnny scattered a good feed on the ground for the horses. He paid his bill, watching the packers, watching the shed, watching all the blind corners of this place.

"Man pass here little while ago?"

The tollkeeper nodded and pointed toward the north. Johnny looked at the hill before him, the long gray folds tumbled together and the trail looping from point to point and disappearing and reappearing again. The sight of it thickened the weariness in his bones. "How long into The Dalles?"

"Ten-twelve hours."

Johnny said, "You know that fellow ahead?"

The tollkeeer said most briefly, "I know him." Then he added, "And he knows me." But this was still not enough, for he again spoke. "You know him?"

"Yes."

"Well, then," said the tollkeeper, and felt he had said everything necessary.

That made it clear, Johnny thought. Since Miller knew that the tollkeeper knew him, he probably wouldn't risk a murder so near witnesses. It was his guess he could climb the canyon without too much risk of ambush; it was only a guess, but he had to go ahead on it. A hopeful thought occurred to him. "That pack outfit going my way?"

"No. South."

Johnny mounted and turned to the trail. Half an hour of steady riding brought him to a series of blind short turns above which the gray parapets of land rose one after another; and the sense of nakedness was upon him once more as he watched those parapets and hugged the high side of the trail. The sun came fully in and the condensed heat sucked moisture out of him until he felt dryness again gluing his throat tissues together. His muscles ached with the tension of waiting for trouble and his nerves were jumpy. When he reached the summit, long afterwards, he faced a country broken into ridges with deep canyons between; he gave the horses a half hour's rest, and stood on his feet to smoke, much too weary to risk lying down. He returned to the saddle with the feeling that he weighed three hundred pounds.

In the middle of the burning afternoon he reached the beginnings of a great hollow which worked its way downward between rising ridge walls. The road went this way, threading the bottom of the hollow and curving out of sight as the hollow turned obediently to the crookedness of the ridges. He followed the road with his doubt growing, meanwhile watching the ridges lift above him, and studying the rocks and the occasional clusters of brush. Three miles of such traveling took him around half a dozen sharp bends and dropped him five hundred feet. He thought, "This is a hell of a place to be in," and considered backing out of the hollow. But his caution could not overcome his weariness; the notion of extra riding was too much and so he continued forward, half listening for the crack of a gun to roll out of some hidden niche in the hills above him. The road curved again and the curve brought him against a gray log hut a hundred yards onward, its roof shakes broken through in places, its door closed and its window staring at him—not a window with its sash, but an open space where a window once had been.

He halted. He drew his gun and he felt the wrongness of the place at once. Why, with the cabin showing the wear and tear of passing travelers, should the door be closed? He kept his eyes on the window square, realizing he could not turn and put his back to it; a rifle bullet would knock him out of the saddle long before he reached the protection of the curve. Neither could he climb the steep ridge and circle the cabin, for on that slope he would be a frozen target.

He got down from the horse and walked forward, the gun lifted and loosely sighted on the window square. The chinking between the logs, he noticed, had begun to fall away but the logs—from this distance—didn't appear to have spaces between them large enough to shoot through. At two hundred feet he began to listen, knowing that if Miller was in the place he'd have his horse with him. He heard nothing. He pushed his feet forward and began to fight the entire weight of that cabin. It shoved him back; it made him use up his strength; it was like walking against a heavy wind.

The sun had dropped behind the western ridge and quick shadows were collecting in the hollow; he felt smaller and smaller underneath the high rims of the ridges, and the empty window square got to be like an eye staring directly at him. His stomach fluttered and grew hollow.

He called out, "Hello—anybody in there?"

His voice rolled around the emptiness. He stooped, never taking his eyes from the window square, and seized a handful of gravel from the road, walnut-sized chunks ground out of the roadbed by the passing freight teams. A hundred feet from the cabin he heaved the rocks at the window square. He missed the opening but he heard the rocks slap the log wall, and suddenly he heard something else—the quick dancing of a disturbed horse inside the cabin. He jumped aside at once and he straightened his aim on the squared window. A shadow moved inside the cabin, and disappeared. Johnny broke into a run, rushing forward and springing aside again. He had thought there could be no moisture left within him after this brutal day, but he began to sweat and his heart slugged him in the ribs. Energy rushed up from somewhere to jolt his muscles into quickness. A gun's report smashed around the inside of the cabin and its bullet scuttered on the road behind Johnny. He saw the shadow moving forward toward the window. He saw Buck Miller stand there, Miller's face half concealed by his risen arm and his slowly aiming gun.

Johnny whipped his shot at the window jumped and dodged, and fired again. Buck Miller's chest and shoulders swayed; the man's gun pulled off and the bullet went wide. Johnny stopped in his tracks. He laid two shots on that swinging torso and saw his target wheel aside. He ran on again and got to the corner of the house, hearing Miller's horse thrashing about the cramped enclosure. Johnny reached the door, lifted the latch and flung it open, he was still in quick motion and ducked back from the door to wait out the shot. None came.

He held himself still for ten or fifteen seconds, or until a great fright made him back away from this side of the house and whirl about, half expecting to find that Buck Miller had gotten through the window and had come around behind him. He kept backing until he caught the two sides of the cabin. He stepped to the right to get a broader view of the cabin through the doorway, and presently he saw a shape, crouched or fallen, in the far corner. He walked toward the doorway, too exhausted to be cautious. The figure didn't move and when he reached the doorway he found Buck Miller on his knees, head and shoulders jammed into the corner. He looked dead.

Johnny caught the horse's cheek strap as it got near the doorway; he pulled it outside and gave it a slap on the rump, then stepped into the cabin and went over to Miller. He moved Miller around by the shoulders and watched him fall over. Miller's hat fell off and he rolled until he lay on his side. This was the fellow who figured that he, Johnny Potter, would run rather than stand up and kill a man. He thought, "How'd he know that much about me? He was right—but how'd he know?" He was sick and he was exhausted; he turned back though the doorway and leaned against the casing a moment to run a hand over his face and to rub away the dry salt and caked dust. His horses were three hundred feet up the road. His knees shook as he walked the distance, his wind gave out on him and he stopped a little while; then he went on and pulled himself into the saddle and started on through the growing twilight.

Even now, knowing he was safe, he found himself watching the shadows and the road with the same tension. It wouldn't break—it had been with him too long; and he reached the hill and rode down a last grade into The Dalles near ten o'clock at night with four days behind him and the watchfulness screwing him tight. Wells Fargo was closed. He had to get the agent's address and go find him and bring him down to the office; he leaned against the desk while the dust was weighed out and took his receipt. He found a stable for the horses, and from there went to the Umatilla House and got a room. He walked into the bar; he had one whiskey quick, and took another to the steam table and ate a meal, and finished with a third whiskey. Then he went to his room, took off his boots and laid his gun under the pillow. He flattened on the bed with nothing over him.

He thought, "Well, it's done and they can buy their damned ranches." He lay still and felt stiffness crawl along his muscles like paralysis, and his eyelids, when he closed them, tortured him with their fiery stinging. The racket of the town came through the window and a small wind shifted the curtain at the window. He opened his eyes, alert to a foreign thing somewhere in the room and searching for it. Finally he saw what troubled him—a small glow of street light passing through the window and touching the wall of the room. The curtain, moved by the wind, shifted the shadow back and forth on the wall. Saddle motion still rocked him and, soothed by this rocking, he fell asleep. It was not a good sleep; it was still the tense and fitful sleep of the trail, with his senses struggling to stay on guard, and quite suddenly the strongest warning struck him and he flung himself out of bed, straight out of his sleep, seized the revolver from beneath the pillow, and fired at the wall.

The roar of the gun woke him completely and he discovered he had put a bullet through the shadow which slid back and forth along the wall. He stared at it a moment, reasoning out his action, as he listened for somebody to come up the stairway on the heels of the shot. But nobody came; apparently this hotel was accustomed to the strange actions of people out of the wild country. He put the gun on the dresser and rolled under the covers and fell so deeply and peacefully asleep that a clap of thunder could not have stirred him.

PRIDE IN HIS HOLSTERS

By ROBERT W. LOWNDES

PRIDE IN HIS HOLSTERS is a first-class pen-portrait of a tired and hopeless gunslick. You'll enjoy this story of Smoke Talbot and his sudden and unexpected act of redemption.

HE was tired of the streets. He rode into Sacaton and the name of the town was something to roll on the tongue, but the glare of the single street was the same. Same saloons, same mercantile, barber shop and hash joints; same line of ponies and rigs hitched on both sides of the street; same boardwalk. And his mission here was the same.

He dismounted, hitched and went into the saloon marked LEARY's, his eyes widening to accommodate themselves to the dimness there. Men at the bar looked up and saw his bright red shirt, saw the wolf-like leanness of him, saw the well-worn holsters on his hips and the guns they contained, and knew him for what he was. Gunman and hired killer; flip-and-toss expert; prideful, the kind that would be sure the other man had a square shake.

He looked around, caring naught for the stares, until his eyes rested on a stocky man sitting alone in a booth to the rear; he strode over and slid in across the table from this one. The man's voice was soft, his hands that had once known calluses from a rope and branding iron were soft; his mid-riff was beginning to bulge. But there was no softness in his eyes; they looked out at the gunman like the eyes of a lizard, small, unblinking, set in deep pouches. The man said, "Talbot?"

"Yeah. You're Jennings."

The other nodded. "You got my message then. Know what you're here for." It wasn't a question.

The bartender came up and put a bottle on the table, shoved shot glasses before both of them. Talbot shook his head. "I'll take beer," he said. "You know my terms." That wasn't a question, either.

He saw the frown creep across the big cowman's face and knew what Jennings was going to say.

Jennings said it. "I don't like to pay half in advance." He made a gesture with his hands. "Suppose—"

"Tough luck, tough for both of us," Talbot cut in. "Tougher on me than you; you'd still be alive and maybe there'd be a cartwheel left on me you could get back. And if you didn't, you could squeeze the dough out of someone else."

Jennings started to take exception and the gunman stood up. "There are other gents who'll do your dirty work." He started to get out of the booth but the other held out a pudgy hand. "All right." He reached into his pocket and took out a billfold. "Two hundred and fifty in advance. You don't have to worry about the law so long as Reardon draws first; I own the law."

"Nice thing to have in your vest pocket. Hell, man, what do you need me for? A frame is cheaper than what I'm costing you and props up your law to boot." There was no anger in Talbot's tones. He'd seen these things too long to care, but he liked to bait the kind of man who'd hire a killer to get rid of someone who stood up to him. And he could spot Jennings' kind with a glance; you could see the greed as clearly as if it had been branded on his forehead.

He got up then, his beer untasted, and stuck the bills into his pocket. "You'll hear from me later," he said and walked out without a backward glance.

He lay on the bed in the cheap hotel room, looking up at the ceiling, and ran over in his mind the information he'd picked up about Johnny Reardon. It was what he had expected; a solid, hard-working man with a will of his own and determination that had brought him up from a drifter to respectability. Wouldn't give an inch when he knew he was in the right; wouldn't turn down a call for help from anyone so long as he had anything to give. Yeah, this was the kind that men like Jennings had to get rid of; you couldn't buy them and you couldn't scare them.

Reardon had one weakness Talbot knew he could use. A temper that flamed when he thought he saw something crooked, particularly in card games. Someone opined that Reardon's father had been shot by a card sharp and that accounted for Johnny's touchiness on this score, but it didn't matter how this had come about. The weakness was there, lurking underneath and waiting to come out, and that was all Talbot needed. Reardon would be in town tonight, in on a stud game.

He slept then, easily, until the light went out of the sky and the glare was gone from the streets. Soft coal-oil lamp-light spilling out of the saloon across from his hotel awakened him. He got up and doused cold water on his face, went downstairs and into a hash joint.

When he came out he heard a woman's voice calling: "Smoke Talbot," and turned around to see her standing in the doorway of the mercantile. He walked across the street and the years seemed to run backward quickly as he came up to her. He looked into Ann Seward's face and the thought of how much he had changed and how little she had was a disturbing thing.

"Still singin', Ann?"

She nodded. A smile crossed her face, the smile he'd known before, as she added, "But not for long, Smoke. I'm getting married next month."

"You should have hit me on the head, Ann. You should have knocked me cold and brought in the sky-pilot. Why didn't you tell me?"

She looked at him levelly and shook her head. "Do you think you would have stayed, Smoke? Young as I was then, I knew better!"

His eyes dropped as he realized the truth in her words; no, he wouldn't have stayed long. He wondered briefly why she wasn't bitter, but another thought crowded this out. A trace of hunger he hadn't realized was in him touched the edges of his words as he said, "You always said you'd name him Pete, Ann. Did you?"

She nodded and he realized that there was a change, after all, something around the eyes that made her look more mature. The thought came to him that she pitied him.

Ann said softly, "He looked a lot like you, Smoke."

Talbot's mouth was suddenly dry. "Is he—"

"There was a flu epidemic that winter; I had it, too.

For a long time I wished the doctor had come a little later. Now I'm glad, Smoke. Someone needs me, someone who's had a hard time and understands a woman like me. I haven't kept anything from him, Smoke, and he still wants me for his wife."

He said harshly, harsh as the thoughts that crossed his mind, "You're marrying Johnny Reardon."

"Yes. Don't go up against him; he'll kill you."

He smiled then, a lean smile that had no humor in it. He looked at her and shrugged slightly. "He might not; I'm pretty fast."

"He'll kill you because he has something to fight for and something to live for. You haven't; all you have is pride in your gunspeed. That isn't enough."

"Suppose he doesn't?"

"Then I will." She said it quietly, then turned away. He watched her walk down the street and something tugged at him, something urged him to go after her. Then the pride in him rose and beat down the weariness, smothered what he wanted to say. He stood for a while, looking out onto the street, then went into Leary's. . . .

Hired gunman and killer. Smoke Talbot studied his cards and said quietly, "I'll keep these." He looked at Reardon across the table from him, and the faces of other men like him who had gone down before Talbot's guns kept coming into his mind. Reardon met his eyes, looked at the stack of chips that had grown in front of the gunman in the past hour; the others had dropped out and only

Talbot and the rancher seemed to be left in the place. "I'll have two," he replied just as quietly.

Talbot pushed a stack of chips out onto the table and Reardon called him. Talbot put his cards down and said matter-of-factly, "Four kings."

Reardon caught Talbot's hand firmly as he started to rake in the chips. "That would make an extra king in the deck, wouldn't it?" He held Talbot's right hand and said, "Don't try a sneak, gun-wolf. The law may be bought and paid for here, but there's some things it can't afford to overlook."

Talbot smiled coldly. "Let go of me, Reardon. I give any man a square shake."

Reardon nodded. "Yeah, your word's good on that, even if you do deal crooked." He gathered up the chips and Talbot smiled.

There was an ache in Talbot's right palm and he knew what would cure it. He said, "You name the place; I'll be there."

Reardon said, "Out in front, at noon." He stood up and put on his hat. "Better spend as much as you can tonight, because you won't need any money after tomorrow."

Talbot watched him go and the realization was sharp in him that Reardon knew what was afoot, that he hadn't waited for the showdown planned. He looked around and saw Jennings beckoning him from a back booth. He nodded, got a bottle from the bar and joined the heavy man.

"Why didn't you get him when the time was right?" Jennings wanted to know. "I told you I own the law."

"Might have known you'd be here watching your investment," Talbot said. "Better walk wide of me after tomorrow, mister, because I might get a touch of sunblindness and mistake you for a snake. Of course, your law would hang me if they got me, but that wouldn't help you any."

"You muffed it," the cattleman said angrily. "You sure damned well muffed it!"

"For your special information," Talbot replied quietly, "I don't shoot under tables. And you'd better not have a stakeout anywhere around tomorrow, because I'm touchy about such things. I might shoot wild and hit the wrong person."

Jennings' lips twitched as he advised Talbot to clear out as soon as the job was done . . .

Flip-and-toss expert. The usual crowd was watching as he started down the street in the noonday sun. He recognized Jennings and saw the man with the star on his shirt across from the rancher. And he knew Ann would be watching.

Prideful. He could tell from the way Reardon wore his guns, from the way the man's hand had grasped him that he, too, could shoot. He started toward the other and the weariness in him was almost alive; it wasn't in his hands, in his arms, in his eyes. But it was there and he thought, Some day it will swallow me. There was no fear attached to his thought, only a certainty.

He saw Jennings out of the corner of his eye, saw the man standing there, licking his lips. Then it was as if a thread had snapped and he was outside of his body, watching with the others. He knew his hand had dropped to his holster in that draw that had beaten the fastest; knew his arm was bringing the gun up before Reardon; knew as well that the shot was high even as he squeezed the trigger. He heard the whine of Reardon's bullet as it passed him, saw the man's gun drop out of his hand as Talbot's slug knocked him backward.

He had time to think: He'll recover, with the nurse he's got. Then his gun was swinging rapidly and Jennings was sinking down, clutching his middle even as the sound of the shot came to his ears.

Talbot felt himself running, zig-zagging as he made for cover. Something slammed into his back and drove the breath out of him. He tried to turn, to lift his gun again, but he knew he was falling. Somehow, somehow his thoughts were sharper than the pain, sharper than the dust in his nostrils.

Then the sun began to go out, and he knew he wouldn't be tired any more. . . .

A MAN CALLED HORSE

By D. M. Johnson

As was said in the general introduction to this book, the
Indian in the old-style Western story was nearly always
a stereotype: a screeching, mindless critter who seemed to
spend most of his time riding around wagon-circles and
getting picked off like a clay pigeon in a shooting-gallery.
Now, here, in the story which follows, is an example of
the modern treatment of the Indian in fiction.

    A MAN CALLED HORSE is a fascinating and exciting story
of Indians as they really lived day by day, and of a white
man who lived among them and earned their respect.
Aside from the gripping story being told, you'll probably
never forget the descriptions of strange and remarkable
Indian customs.

HE was a young man of good family, as the phrase went
in the New England of a hundred-odd years ago, and the
reasons for his bitter discontent were unclear, even to himself. He grew up in the gracious old Boston home under
his grandmother's care, for his mother had died in giving
him birth; and all his life he had known every comfort and
privilege his father's wealth could provide.

    But still there was the discontent, which puzzled him
because he could not even define it. He wanted to live
among his equals—people who were no better than he and
no worse either. That was as close as he could come to
describing the source of his unhappiness in Boston and his
restless desire to go somewhere else.

In the year 1845, he left home and went out West, far beyond the country's creeping frontier, where he hoped to find his equals. He had the idea that in Indian country, where there was danger, all white men were kings, and he wanted to be one of them. But he found, in the West as in Boston, that the men he respected were still his superiors, even if they could not read, and those he did not respect weren't worth talking to.

He did have money, however, and he could hire the men he respected. He hired four of them, to cook and hunt and guide and be his companions, but he found them not friendly.

They were apart from him and he was still alone. He still brooded about his status in the world, longing for his equals.

On a day in June, he learned what it was to have no status at all. He became a captive of a small riding party of Crow Indians.

He heard gunfire and the brief shouts of his companions around the bend of the creek just before they died, but he never saw their bodies. He had no chance to fight, because he was naked and unarmed, bathing in the creek, when a Crow warrior seized and held him.

His captor let him go at last, let him run. Then the lot of them rode him down for sport, striking him with their coup sticks. They carried the dripping scalps of his companions, and one had skinned off Baptiste's black beard as well, for a trophy.

They took him along in a matter-of-fact way, as they took the captured horses. He was unshod and naked as the horses were, and like them he had a rawhide thong around his neck. So long as he didn't fall down, the Crows ignored him.

On the second day they gave him his breeches. His feet were too swollen for his boots, but one of the Indians threw him a pair of moccasins that had belonged to the halfbreed, Henry, who was dead back at the creek. The captive wore the moccasins gratefully. The third day they let him ride one of the spare horses so the party could move faster, and on that day they came in sight of their camp.

He thought of trying to escape, hoping he might be killed in flight rather than by slow torture in the camp, but he never had a chance to try. They were more familiar with escape than he was and, knowing what to expect, they forestalled it. The only other time he had tried to escape from anyone, he had succeeded. When he had left his home in Boston, his father had raged and his grandmother had cried, but they could not talk him out of his intention.

The men of the Crow raiding party didn't bother with talk.

Before riding into camp they stopped and dressed in their regalia, and in parts of their victims' clothing; they painted their faces black. Then, leading the white man by the rawhide around his neck as though he were a horse, they rode down toward the tepee circle, shouting and singing, brandishing their weapons. He was unconscious when they got there; he fell and was dragged.

He lay dazed and battered near a tepee while the noisy,

busy life of the camp swarmed around him and Indians came to stare. Thirst consumed him, and when it rained he lapped rain water from the ground like a dog. A scrawny, shrieking, eternally busy old woman with ragged graying hair threw a chunk of meat on the grass, and he fought the dogs for it.

When his head cleared, he was angry, although anger was an emotion he knew he could not afford.

It was better when I was a horse, he thought—when they led me by the rawhide around my neck. I won't be a dog, no matter what!

The hag gave him stinking, rancid grease and let him figure out what it was for. He applied it gingerly to his bruised and sun-seared body.

Now, he thought, I smell like the rest of them.

While he was healing, he considered coldly the advantages of being a horse. A man would be humiliated, and sooner or later he would strike back and that would be the end of him. But a horse had only to be docile. Very well, he would learn to do without pride.

He understood that he was the property of the screaming old woman, a fine gift from her son, one that she liked to show off. She did more yelling at him than at anyone else, probably to impress the neighbors so they would not forget what a great and generous man her son was. She was bossy and proud, a dreadful sag of skin and bones, and she was a devilish hard worker.

The white man, who now thought of himself as a horse, forgot sometimes to worry about his danger. He kept making mental notes of things to tell his own people in

Boston about this hideous adventure. He would go back a hero and he would say, "Grandmother, let me fetch your shawl. I've been accustomed to doing little errands for another lady about your age."

Two girls lived in the tepee with the old hag and her warrior son. One of them, the white man concluded, was his captors' wife and the other was his little sister. The daughter-in-law was smug and spoiled. Being beloved, she did not have to be useful. The younger girl had bright, wandering eyes. Often enough they wandered to the white man who was pretending to be a horse.

The two girls worked when the old woman put them at it, but they were always running off to do something they enjoyed more. There were games and noisy contests, and there was much laughter. But not for the white man. He was finding out what loneliness could be.

That was a rich summer on the plains, with plenty of buffalo for meat and clothing and the making of tepees. The Crows were wealthy in horses, prosperous and contented. If their men had not been so avid for glory, the white man thought, there would have been a lot more of them. But they went out of their way to court death, and when one of them met it, the whole camp mourned extravagantly and cried to their God for vengeance.

The captive was a horse all summer, a docile bearer of burdens, careful and patient. He kept reminding himself that he had to be better-natured than other horses, because he could not lash out with hoofs or teeth. Helping the old woman load up the horses for travel, he yanked at a pack and said, "Whoa, brother. It goes easier when you don't fight."

The horse gave him a big-eyed stare as if it understood his language—a comforting thought, because nobody else did. But even among the horses he felt unequal. They were able to look out for themselves if they escaped. He would simply starve. He was envious still, even among the horses.

Humbly he fetched and carried. Sometimes he even offered to help, but he had not the skill for the endless work of the women, and he was not trusted to hunt with the men, the providers.

When the camp moved, he carried a pack, trudging with the women. Even the dogs worked then, pulling small burdens on travois of sticks.

The Indian who had captured him lived like a lord, as he had a right to do. He hunted with his peers, attended long ceremonial meetings with much chanting and dancing, and lounged in the shade with his smug bride. He had only two responsibilities: to kill buffalo and to gain glory. The white man was so far beneath him in status that the Indian did not even think of envy.

One day several things happened that made the captive think he might sometime become a man again. That was the day when he began to understand their language. For four months he had heard it, day and night, the joy and the mourning, the ritual chanting and sung prayers, the squabbles and the deliberation. None of it meant anything to him at all.

But on that important day in early fall the two young

women set out for the river, and one of them called over her shoulder to the old woman. The white man was startled. She had said she was going to bathe. His understanding was so sudden that he felt as if his ears had come unstopped. Listening to the racket of the camp, he heard fragments of meaning instead of gabble.

On that same important day the old woman brought a pair of new moccasins out of the tepee and tossed them on the ground before him. He could not believe she would do anything for him because of kindness, but giving him moccasins was one way of looking after her property.

In thanking her, he dared greatly. He picked a little handful of fading fall flowers and took them to her as she squatted in front of her tepee, scraping a buffalo hide with a tool made from a piece of iron tied to a bone. Her hands were hideous—most of the fingers had the first joint missing. He bowed solemnly and offered the flowers.

She glared at him from beneath the short ragged tangle of her hair. She stared at the flowers, knocked them out of his hand and went running to the next tepee, squalling the story. He heard her and the other women screaming with laughter.

The white man squared his shoulders and walked boldly over to watch three small boys shooting arrows at a target. He said in English, "Show me how to do that, will you?"

They frowned, but he held out his hand as if there could be no doubt. One of them gave him a bow and one arrow, and they snickered when he missed.

The people were easily amused, except when they were angry. They were amused, at him, playing with the little boys. A few days later he asked the hag, with gestures, for a bow that her son had just discarded, a man-size bow of horn. He scavenged for old arrows. The old woman cackled at his marksmanship and called her neighbors to enjoy the fun.

When he could understand words, he could identify his people by their names. The old woman was Greasy Hand, and her daughter was Pretty Calf. The other young woman's name was not clear to him, for the words were not in his vocabulary. The man who had captured him was Yellow Robe.

Once he could understand, he could begin to talk a little, and then he was less lonely. Nobody had been able to see any reason for talking to him, since he would not understand anyway. He asked the old woman, "What is my name?" Until he knew it, he was incomplete. She shrugged to let him know he had none.

He told her in the Crow language, "My name is Horse." He repeated it, and she nodded. After that they called him Horse when they called him anything. Nobody cared except the white man himself.

They trusted him enough to let him stray out of camp, so that he might have got away and, by unimaginable good luck, might have reached a trading post or a fort, but winter was too close. He did not dare leave without a horse; he needed clothing and a better hunting weapon than he had, and more certain skill in using it. He did not dare steal, for then they would surely have pursued him, and just as certainly they would have caught him. Remembering the warmth of the home that was waiting in Boston, he settled down for the winter.

On a cold night he crept into the tepee after the others had gone to bed. Even a horse might try to find shelter from the wind. The old woman grumbled, but without conviction. She did not put him out.

They tolerated him, back in the shadows, so long as he did not get in the way.

He began to understand how the family that owned him differed from the others. Fate had been cruel to them. In a short, sharp argument among the old women, one of them derided Greasy Hand by sneering, "You have no relatives!" and Greasy Hand raved for minutes of the deeds of her father and uncles and brothers. And she had had four sons, she reminded her detractor—who answered with scorn, "Where are they?"

Later the white man found her moaning and whimpering to herself, rocking back and forth on her haunches, staring at her mutilated hands. By that time he understood. A mourner often chopped off a finger joint. Old Greasy Hand had mourned often. For the first time he felt a twinge of pity, but he put it aside as another emotion, like anger, that he could not afford. He thought: What tales I will tell when I get home!

He wrinkled his nose in disdain. The camp stank of animals and meat and rancid grease. He looked down at his naked, shivering legs and was startled, remembering that he was still only a horse.

He could not trust the old woman. She fed him only because a starved slave would die and not be worth boasting about. Just how fitful her temper was he saw on the day when she got tired of stumbling over one of the hundred dogs that infested the camp. This was one of her own dogs, a large, strong one that pulled a baggage travois when the tribe moved camp.

Countless times he had seen her kick at the beast as it lay sleeping in front of the tepee, in her way. The dog always moved, with a yelp, but it always got in the way again. One day she gave the dog its usual kick and then stood scolding at it while the animal rolled its eyes sleepily. The old woman suddenly picked up her ax and cut the dog's head half off with one blow. Looking well satisfied with herself, she beckoned her slave to remove the body.

It could have been me, he thought, if I were a dog. I'm a horse.

His hope of life lay with the girl, Pretty Calf. He set about courting her, realizing how desperately poor he was both in property and honor. He owned no horse, no weapon but the old bow and the battered arrows. He had nothing to give away, and he needed gifts, because he did not dare seduce the girl.

One of the customs of courtship involved sending a gift of horses to a girl's older brother and bestowing much buffalo meat upon her mother. The white man could not wait for some far-off time when he might have either horses or meat to give away. And his courtship had to be secret. It was not for him to stroll past the groups of watchful girls, blowing a flute made of an eagle's wing bone, as the flirtatious young bucks did.

He could not ride past Pretty Calf's tepee, painted and bedizened; he had no horses, no finery.

Back home, he remembered, I could marry just about any girl I'd want to. But he wasted little time thinking about that. A future was something to be earned.

The most he dared do was wink at Pretty Calf now and then, or state his admiration, while she giggled and hid her face. The least he dared do to win his bride was to elope with her, but he had to give her a horse to put the seal of tribal approval on that. And he had no horse until he killed a man to get one. . . .

His opportunity came in early spring. He was casually accepted by that time. He did not belong, but he was amusing to the Crows, like a strange pet, or they would not have fed him through the winter.

His chance came when he was hunting small game with three young boys who were his guards as well as his scornful companions. Rabbits and birds were of no account in a camp well fed on buffalo meat, but they made good targets.

His party walked far that day. All of them at once saw the two horses in a sheltered coulee. The boys and the man crawled forward on their bellies, and then they saw an Indian who lay on the ground, moaning, a lone traveler. From the way the boys inched eagerly forward, Horse knew the man was fair prey—a member of some enemy tribe.

This is the way the captive white man acquired wealth and honor to win a bride and save his life: He shot an arrow into the sick man, a split second ahead of one of his small companions, and dashed forward to strike the still-groaning man with his bow, to count first coup. Then he seized the hobbled horses.

By the time he had the horses secure, and with them his hope for freedom, the boys had followed, counting coup with gestures and shrieks they had practiced since boyhood, and one of them had the scalp. The white man was grimly amused to see the boy double up with sudden nausea when he had the thing in his hand. . . .

There was a hubbub in the camp when they rode in that evening, two of them on each horse. The captive was noticed. Indians who had ignored him as a slave stared at the brave man who had struck first coup and had stolen horses.

The hubbub lasted all night, as fathers boasted loudly of their young sons' exploits. The white man was called upon to settle an argument between two fierce boys as to which of them had struck second coup and which must be satisfied with third. After much talk that went over his head, he solemnly pointed at the nearest boy. He didn't know which boy it was and didn't care, but the boy did.

The white man had watched warriors in their triumph. He knew what to do. Modesty about achievements had no place among the Crow people. When a man did something big, he told about it.

The white man smeared his face with grease and charcoal. He walked inside the tepee circle, chanting and sing-ing. He used his own langauge.

"You heathens, you savages," he shouted. "I'm going to get out of here someday! I am going to get away!" The Crow people listened respectfully. In the Crow tongue he shouted. "Horse! I am Horse!" and they nod-ded.

He had a right to boast, and he had two horses. Before dawn, the white man and his bride were sheltered beyond a far hill, and he was telling her, "I love you, little lady. I love you."

She looked at him with her great dark eyes, and he thought she understood English words—or as much as she needed to understand.

"You are my treasure," he said, "more precious than jewels, better than fine gold. I am going to call you Freedom."

When they returned to camp two days later, he was bold but worried. His ace, he suspected, might not be high enough in the game he was playing without being sure of the rules. But it served.

Old Greasy Hand raged—but not at him. She com-plained loudly that her daughter had let herself go too cheap. But the marriage was as good as any Crow mar-riage. He had paid a horse.

He learned the language faster after that, from Pretty Calf, whom he sometimes called Freedom. He learned that his attentive, adoring bride was fourteen years old.

One thing he had not guessed was the difference that being Pretty Calf's husband would make in his relationship to her mother and brother. He had hoped only to make his position a little safer, but he had not expected to be treated with dignity. Greasy Hand no longer spoke to him at all. When the white man spoke to her, his bride murmured in dismay, explaining at great length that he must never do that. There could be no conversation between a man and his mother-in-law. He could not even mention a word that was part of her name.

Having improved his status so magnificently, he felt no need for hurry in getting away. Now that he had a woman, he had as good a chance to be rich as any man. Pretty Calf waited on him; she seldom ran off to play games with other young girls, but took pride in learning from her mother the many women's skills of tanning hides and making clothing and preparing food.

He was no more a horse but a kind of man, a half-Indian, still poor and unskilled but laden with honors, clinging to the buckskin fringes of Crow society.

Escape could wait until he could manage it in comfort, with fit clothing and a good horse, with hunting weapons. Escape could wait until the camp moved near some trading post. He did not plan how he would get home. He dreamed of being there all at once, and of telling stories nobody would believe. There was no hurry.

Pretty Calf delighted in educating him. He began to understand tribal arrangements, customs and why things were as they were. They were that way because they had always been so. His young wife giggled when she told him, in his ignorance, things she had always known. But she did not laugh when her brother's wife was taken by another warrior. She explained that solemnly with words and signs.

Yellow Robe belonged to a society called the Big Dogs. The wife stealer, Cut Neck, belonged to the Foxes. They were fellow tribesmen; they hunted together and fought side by side, but men of one society could take away wives from the other society if they wished, subject to certain limitations.

When Cut Neck rode up to the tepee, laughing and singing, and called to Yellow Robe's wife, "Come out! Come out!" she did as ordered, looking smug as usual, meek and entirely willing. Thereafter she rode beside him in ceremonial processions and carried his coup stick, while his other wife pretended not to care.

"But why?" the white demanded of his wife, his Freedom. "Why did our brother let his woman go? He sits and smokes and does not speak."

Pretty Calf was shocked at the suggestion. Her brother could not possibly reclaim his woman, she explained. He could not even let her come back if she wanted to—and she probably would want to when Cut Neck tired of her. Yellow Robe could not even admit that his heart was sick. That was the way things were. Deviation meant dishonor.

The woman could have hidden from Cut Neck, she said. She could even have refused to go with him if she had been *ba-wurokee*—a really virtuous woman. But she had been his woman before, for a little while on a berrying expedition, and he had a right to claim her.

There was no sense in it, the white man insisted. He

glared at his young wife. "If you go, I will bring you back!" he promised.

She laughed and buried her head against his shoulder. "I will not have to go," she said. "Horse is my first man. There is no hole in my moccasin."

He stroked her hair and said, *"Ba-wurokee."*

With great daring, she murmured, *"Hay-ha,"* and when he did not answer, because he did not know what she meant, she drew away hurt.

"A woman calls her man that if she thinks he will not leave her. Am I wrong?"

The white man held her closer and lied. "Pretty Calf is not wrong. Horse will not leave her. Horse will not take another woman, either." No. he certainly would not. Parting from this one was going to be harder than getting her had been. *"Hay-ha,"* he murmured. "Freedom."

His conscience irked him, but not very much. Pretty Calf could get another man easily enough when he was gone, and a better provider. His hunting skill was improving, but he was still awkward.

There was no hurry about leaving. He was used to most of the Crow ways and could stand the rest. He was becoming prosperous. He owned five horses. His place in the life of the tribe was secure, such as it was. Three or four young women, including the one who had belonged to Yellow Robe, made advances to him. Pretty Calf took pride in the fact that her man was so attractive.

By the time he had what he needed for a secret journey, the grass grew yellow on the plains and the long cold was close. He was enslaved by the girl he called Freedom and, before the winter ended, by the knowledge that she was carrying his child. . . .

The Big Dog society held a long ceremony in the spring. The white man strolled with his woman along the creek bank, thinking: When I get home I will tell them about the chants and the drumming. Sometime. Sometime.

Pretty Calf would not go to bed when they went back to the tepee.

"Wait and find out about my brother," she urged. "Something may happen."

So far as Horse could figure out, the Big Dogs were having some kind of election. He pampered his wife by staying up with her by the fire. Even the old woman, who was a great one for getting sleep when she was not working, prowled around restlessly.

The white man was yawning by the time the noise of the ceremony died down. When Yellow Robe strode in, garish and heathen in his paint and feathers and furs, the women cried out. There was conversation, too fast for Horse to follow, and the old woman wailed once, but her son silenced her with a gruff command.

When the white man went to sleep, he thought his wife was weeping beside him.

The next morning she explained.

"He wears the bearskin belt. Now he can never retreat in battle. He will always be in danger. He will die."

Maybe he wouldn't, the white man tried to convince her. Pretty Calf recalled that some few men had been honored by the bearskin belt, vowed to the highest daring, and had not died. If they lived through the summer, then they were free of it.

"My brother wants to die," she mourned. "His heart is bitter."

Yellow Robe lived through half a dozen clashes with small parties of raiders from hostile tribes. His honors were many. He captured horses in an enemy camp, led two successful raids, counted first coup and snatched a gun from the hand of an enemy tribesman. He wore wolf tails on his moccasins and ermine skins on his shirt, and he fringed his leggings with scalps in token of his glory.

When his mother ventured to suggest, as she did many times, "My son should take a new wife, I need another woman to help me," he ignored her. He spent much time in prayer, alone in the hills or in conference with a medicine man. He fasted and made vows and kept them. And before he could be free of the heavy honor of the bearskin belt, he went on his last raid.

The warriors were returning from the north just as the white man and two other hunters approached from the south, with buffalo and elk meat dripping from the bloody hides tied on their restive ponies. One of the hunters grunted, and they stopped to watch a rider on the hill north of the tepee circle.

The rider dismounted, held up a blanket and dropped it. He repeated the gesture.

The hunters murmured dismay. "Two! Two men dead!" They rode fast into the camp where there was already wailing.

A messenger came down from the war party on the hill. The rest of the party delayed to paint their faces for mourning and for victory. One of the two dead men was Yellow Robe. They had put his body in a cave and walled it in with rocks. The other man died later, and his body was in a tree.

There was blood on the ground before the tepee to which Yellow Robe would return no more. His mother, with her hair chopped short, sat in the doorway, rocking back and forth on her haunches, wailing her heartbreak. She cradled one mutilated hand in the other. She had cut off another finger joint.

Pretty Calf had cut off chunks of her long hair and was crying as she gashed her arms with a knife. The white man tried to take the knife away, but she protested so piteously that he let her do as she wished. He was sickened with the lot of them.

Savages! he thought. Now I will go back! I'll go hunting alone, and I'll keep going.

But he did not go just yet, because he was the only hunter in the lodge of the two grieving women, one of them old and the other pregnant with his child.

In their mourning, they made him a pauper again. Everything that meant comfort, wealth and safety they sacrificed to the spirits because of the death of Yellow Robe. The tepee, made of seventeen fine buffalo hides, the furs that should have kept them warm, the white deerskin dress, trimmed with elk teeth, that Pretty Calf loved so well, even their tools and Yellow Robe's weapons—everything but his sacred medicine objects—they left there on

128

the prairie, and the whole camp moved away. Two of his best horses were killed as a sacrifice, and the women gave away the rest.

They had no shelter. They would have no tepee of their own for two months at least of mourning, and the women would have to tan hides to make it. Meanwhile they could live in temporary huts made of willows, covered with skins given them in pity by their friends. They could have lived with relatives, but Yellow Robe's women had no relatives.

The white man had not realized until then how terrible a thing it was for a Crow to have no kinfolk. No wonder old Greasy Hand had only stumps for fingers. She had mourned, from one year to the next, for everyone she had ever loved. She had no one left but her daughter, Pretty Calf.

Horse was furious at their foolishness. It had been bad enough for him, a captive, to be naked as a horse and poor as a slave, but that was because his captors had stripped him. These women had voluntarily given up everything they needed.

He was too angry at them to sleep in the willow hut. He lay under a sheltering tree. And on the third night of the mourning he made his plans. He had a knife and a bow. He would go after meat, taking two horses. And he would not come back. There were, he realized, many things he was not going to tell when he got back home.

In the willow hut, Pretty Calf cried out. He heard rustling there, and the old woman's querulous voice.

Some twenty hours later his son was born, two months

early, in the tepee of a skilled medicine woman. The child was born without breath, and the mother died before the sun went down.

The white man was too shocked to think whether he should mourn, or how he should mourn. The old woman screamed until she was voiceless. Piteously she approached him, bent and trembling, blind with grief. She held out her knife and he took it.

She spread out her hands and shook her head. If she cut off any more finger joints, she could do no more work. She could not afford any more lasting signs of grief.

The white man said, "All right! All right!" between his teeth. He hacked his arms with the knife and stood watching the blood run down. It was little enough to do for Pretty Calf, for little Freedom.

Now there is nothing to keep me, he realized. When I get home, I must not let them see the scars.

He looked at Greasy Hand, hideous in her grief-burdened age, and thought: I really am free now! When a wife dies, her husband has no more duty toward her family. Pretty Calf had told him so, long ago, when he wondered why a certain man moved out of one tepee and into another.

The old woman, of course, would be a scavenger. There was one other with the tribe, an ancient crone who had no relatives, toward whom no one felt any responsibility. She lived on food thrown away by the more fortunate. She slept in shelters that she built with her own knotted hands. She plodded wearily at the end of the procession when the camp moved. When she stumbled nobody cared. When she died, nobody would miss her.

Tomorrow morning, the white man decided, I will go.

His mother-in-law's sunken mouth quivered. She said one word, questioningly. She said, "*Eero-oshay?*" She said, "Son?"

Blinking, he remembered. When a wife died, her husband was free. But her mother, who had ignored him with dignity, might if she wished ask him to stay. She invited him by calling him Son, and he accepted by answering Mother.

Greasy Hand stood before him, bowed with years, withered with unceasing labor, loveless and childless, scarred with grief. But with all her burdens, she still loved life enough to beg it from him, the only person she had any right to ask. She was stripping herself of all she had left, her pride.

He looked eastward across the prairie. Two thousand miles away was home. The old woman would not live forever. He could afford to wait, for he was young. He could afford to be magnanimous, for he knew he was a man. He gave her the answer. "*Eegya,*" he said. "Mother."

He went home three years later. He explained no more than to say, "I lived with Crows for a while. It was some time before I could leave. They called me Horse."

He did not find it necessary either to apologize or to boast, because he was the equal of any man on earth.

THE GHOST LODE

By William Brandon

THE GHOST LODE is a story of gold fever—of what happens
to an old prospector when he sees a chance to realize his
life-long dreams of wealth. Ask yourself this question
when you finish the story: would *you* have let the delirious youngster die?

THE desert lay like a rug at the foot of the gaunt, gray
mountains. The shadows of the night ran from it and
dissolved in the ivory daylight, and waking quail talked
sleepily from their mesquite roosts. The rising sun opened
a golden fan across the sky, and the quail moved out in
vast, softly whirring clouds and settled to the ground to
feed.

Sunlight touched the mountain peaks a mile above and
fell like a gilded curtain from the rims and cliffs and ridges
to the deep, green canyons, where little dun-colored deer
with velvet antlers paused to lift their heads and watch.
Now the sun stood on end on the edge of the world, and
glittering rivers of sunlight raced across the land, melting
the last of the cold night air, breathing the heat of the day.

An old man and two burros threaded their way through
the chaparral. The landscape all about them was splashed
with the vivid paint of countless flowers, masses of scarlet
ocotillo and yellow paloverde and the giant incandescent
yucca that the *paisanos* called the Candle of God. On the
higher mesas great seas of field flowers ran in rainbow
waves before the morning wind.

From time to time the old man killed a quail with a rusty shotgun. The muzzle blast of the gun echoed for minutes, it seemed, in the immensity of space. The quail fled rustling through the brush, chirping in terror, but they did not fly.

The old man's eyes were bright and lively. A stubble of silver beard masked his face. His clothes and his ragged hat were streaked with sweat and dust. He wore a length of rope for a belt. He talked to the blue quail as he killed them and stuffed them in his pocket:

"Shake your topknot at me, will you. . . . Look there, now, your breast all tore up. Wasn't that a bum shot, though? . . . You'll sing for me in the skillet, mister. That ain't a bad go, is it?"

The burros stopped suddenly, heads up and ears wigwagging, and refused to go on.

"Now, what in tarnation?" the old man said. "The day ain't hardly started yet—you going to begin making trouble already? Hey, get along now!"

The burros were named (after a pair of minstrel men of the old man's youth) Hasdrubal and Hamilcar. They looked frail under their packs. They heaved their gray, moth-eaten flanks in unison. Their eyes were wan and philosophical. The old man swatted Hasdrubal's bony rump with the shotgun, but the burro only humped his back and hiked a leg to kick.

"All right, baby, all right, we'll see. Old Dad will see what you're scared of, and it blamed well better be something." He called to a quail perched on a flower-covered cactus, "Cordonisito, what do you see yonder?"

The little quail looked at him with disconcerting directness, his topknot dangling over one eye, and then hopped down to the ground and disappeared.

The old man walked ahead, looking here and there. He peered through the brush, and saw a man sitting on the ground only a few feet away, watching him.

"Why, holy smoke!" the old man said. He spoke out sternly, but without moving from behind the greasewood that screened him, "Hey, you, young fella!"

The young man looked at him, smiling, but did not answer. He was hatless. His hair was black and shaggy. He sat in an attitude of complete exhaustion, his legs sprawled out, his shoulders bowed, his hands resting palm up in the dust. His smile did not waver and his watching eyes scarcely seemed to blink.

The old man swallowed. Everyone knew there were creatures out here that could take any form they pleased. The young man smiled on, never moving. After a time the old man said suddenly, "By golly, boys, I believe he's dead."

He walked up cautiously to the black-haired young man and touched him, and the young man swayed and fell on his side. But he was not dead. One arm moved, and the black head, after a moment, turned a little, as if to nuzzle into the warm comfort of the sand.

The old man knelt over him and felt the fast, faint beat of his heart, and brought his hand away smeared with black blood. He pulled off the young man's shirt and saw a gunshot wound through his body. The bullet had smashed into his lower ribs and come out the small of his back, where it had left a gaping purple eruption. The smile on his face, the old man saw now, was a frozen grimace of pain. The expression in his eyes was the fixed, tranquil stare of coma.

He was as good as dead already, the old man knew, but he thought he would do what he could for him. He brought the packs from his burros, made a fire and boiled water, cleaned the two wounds of dirt and pus and bits of shattered bone, and bound them up. He rolled out his own bed for the wounded man and staked up a trap for a sunshade.

"You might as well die in style, boy," he said. "That's more'n most of us will get."

When he straightened the young man out on the blankets he found the leather bags of gold. There were two of them, flat saddlebags, strung by thongs to the wounded man's belt. When the old man opened them he poured from each a double handful of ore samples.

"Well, now," the old man said, in a whisper of awe.

The bits of rock were of a richness he would not have believed possible. Why, dirt like this, he thought would assay five hundred fine straight from the pick and shovel. It wasn't ore, it was solid gold!

He looked from the gold to the wounded man with a totally new interest and excitement. The boy's breath whistled faintly in his throat and his half-closed eyes smiled mysteriously at the tarpaulin overhead.

"This tells a story," the old man said, "And don't I wish I knew it?"

He studied the ore for a long while, and kept it before him while he ate his noon meal of quail and coffee. The lode it had been dug from would surely be the richest strike in the world. The old man had found pay streaks in his time, but never anything to come close to this. He had dreamed all his life of something like the fabulous, free milling-ledge these samples must represent.

He returned the samples to the two saddlebags finally, and stowed them deep in one of his packs.

The wounded man's lips moved to a taste of water.

"Where'd you find it, son?" the old man asked softly.

He listened, and heard only the labored breathing. It was weaker, he thought. Very likely the boy would not live till sundown.

The old man settled himself and stayed close by, with the thought that the boy might possibly come to himself for a minute before he died, and talk.

The sun filled the world with white, quivering, smothering heat, and the dazzling color of the flowered desert danced and leaped, while the quail all about cried incessantly, "He's got the gold! He's got the gold!" The sun sat upon the mountains like a pot of burning brass. Evening shadows stole across the flats and the sun slid suddenly from sight. Rails of gold and silver stretched across the sky and slowly faded away, and the afterglow flared in the east. The old man made up his fire again.

He tried feeding the wounded man with a spoonful of broth cooked from the bones of the quail.

The boy swallowed the broth and feebly worked his tongue.

The old man said coaxingly, "What's that? What's that you say, son?"

". . . Bill Jones . . ."

"Sure, sure; go on. Bill Jones, you say? Pleased to know you, Bill. My name's Ben—Ben Sandy, they call me, although that ain't my name, but that's no matter; Crazy Ben Sandy some folks say when they want to get my goat. They think any man's crazy will live and die out here. You got something else to say, Bill? You locate something up in the hills, did you, Bill? Seems to me I seen some high-grade ore. You remember, son? Can you remember?"

Bill Jones said nothing. His eyes were entirely closed now and his sunburned face looked like death, but the old man touched his pulse and felt it drumming madly on.

The old man sighed. Death was standing by, nevertheless, and would surely step into the camp before morning. But Bill Jones had spoken once. He might, still, talk again.

It was easy enough to cipher out a great part of the story, the old man thought. Bill Jones had gone prospecting in the mountains with a partner. They had made this strike, this bonanza pocket of infinite riches, enough to make any man lose his senses. Rich enough to give you a fortune for every day's work, rich as the Ghost Lode itself. So they had no more than located it before they had turned suspicious of each other, crazy with gold madness as they would have been. They had fallen into a row, and one of them had gone for the other with a gun. Bill Jones

137

had killed his partner, but he had gotten a bullet through him while he was about it. He had lived long enough to wander this far (from where?) and now he, too, was dying.

That Bill Jones had killed his partner the old man was reasonably certain, because Bill Jones was carrying the samples with him. The saddlebags of ore would naturally have gone to the victor.

Night fell. Coyotes yapped in the hills, and a cactus rat worked tirelessly near by on his house of cholla joints. The burros came close to the fire to doze. Stars flowed in glittering streams across the sky. The mountains towered among the stars, black and gigantic and silent.

The Ghost Lode returned to the old man's thoughts, and an uneasiness ran through his bones.

The story of the Ghost Lode had been old before Ben Sandy was born. No one had ever found it. No one ever saw anything of it except a load of pure raw gold, alike enough, the old man supposed, to the samples Bill Jones had been carrying. Although there would be a good deal more of it, he guessed, hundreds of pounds, a burro-load or so, enough to be a fortune in itself. But the story, as it was told, held that no man could live to bring in the Ghost Lode gold.

The Ghost Lode led men to death. Worse, it led them to murder, which meant they lost their souls before they lost their lives. Its bewitched gold went eternally from hand to hand, the story related, and to possess it was to die. But, so the story said, you could possess it only by killing the previous owner. That was where you lost your soul.

After that you missed your way, your mules sickened and died, your water gave out, and then the next man found you. And when the gold from the Ghost Lode set his brain on fire, then it was your time to die, and the gold traveled on.

Plenty of men had dropped out of sight in these mountains. Ben had known many. Who was to say the Ghost Lode was a myth? The old man had once been young enough to laugh at the story. The young are natural skeptics. When you are young you think death itself a myth. But the old man had been too long alone, with time for thought, and he had seen too many strange things.

There had been a girl once, a long time ago, and the old man had almost married her, but she had died of the smallpox. Now, he had seen her many times since, in the desert. She would come running toward him and stop a little way off and then hold out her hands, and then she would be gone. In his own head? Maybe, but Hamilcar and Hasdrubal saw her, too. They would stop stock-still and watch.

The burros saw her as the burros heard the voices that the old man heard. The voices, the scattered words of people from days long gone, people the old man had known or people the desert only had known, the voices dwelt forever in certain secret places. Who would prove they were only the wind? . . . .

The old man wakened with a start. The fire was dead and the stars were dim. Bill Jones was talking in a hoarse and fretful whisper. The old man moved on his aching legs and bent close to listen.

". . . old Bill Jones . . ."

"All right, Bill. Go ahead. Tell me what you want to say."

The wounded man opened his mouth and drew in a long, shuddering breath.

"Now he's dying," the old man thought angrily. But a thread of pulse still clung to life. The old man crouched beside him waiting, and presently fell asleep again.

In the morning Bill Jones was still alive. He was young and well-muscled and strong, and so death was having a long wait for him, but it was impossible, the old man thought, that he could last through the day.

"Sure can't be no Ghost Lode," the old man told his burros. "He's dying fast enough of his own self without any help from me."

Hamilcar drew back his lips and wheezed through yellow teeth.

"I'm doing the best I can to keep him alive," the old man pointed out. "Ain't that so? You never knew me to do harm to anyone yet, did you? Not my style, boys; you know that. But I sure wish he'd come to for just five minutes."

He would have liked to stay on in camp, in case Bill Jones should talk again and say something worth hearing, but his water was running too low. He had used a lot of it for the wounded man. He took the burros and packed on to the mountains to refill his kegs.

He followed Bill Jones's back trail as long as he could

make it out. It wandered erratically across the dreamlike desert gardens, among the fantastic flowers. At one point he found a discarded canteen. Then the trail skirted a mesa, through a broken country slashed with blood-red gullies, and here the last traces of tracks disappeared.

Later, on the mesa, he killed another mess of quail. The birds did not run from him through the grass, but flushed and sailed away over fields of waving poppies. It was unusual for these birds to fly, back here where they were never hunted.

The wide tableland was split across its middle with a deep arroyo, as though by the stroke of a giant ax. The arroyo ran to the base of the mountains, where its wash, strewn with boulders and a vast float of rubble, angled into a shallow stream. The creek was now more dry than wet, but the old man found water enough in its potholes.

He returned along the arroyo clear to the flats and went back to camp by a different route, hoping to cut further sign of Bill Jones's trail. He saw nothing.

He was a hundred yards from his camp when he heard Bill Jones's voice raised in a yell. The old man broke into a frantic run, and pounded into camp out of breath and with his blood booming in his ears.

The wounded man greeted him with delirious exuberance. His face was a bright red and his eyes gleamed like fire.

The old man dropped to his knees beside him. He gasped, "What's that you say, Bill? What was you saying, boy?"

"... *Old Bill Jones ... had two daughters and a song ...*"

The boy was singing. His voice rolled lustily across the stillness of the afternoon.

"... *Old Bill Jones had two daughters and a song,*
One went to Denver and the other went wrong ..."

The old man, after a time, got up and brought him a drink of water. Bill Jones knocked the cup aside. The water flew glistening through the air.

"... *His wife she died in a poolroom fight,*
But still he sings from morning till night ..."

Bill Jones groaned and his back stiffened in a convulsion of agony. The old man reached out and held his shoulders. He could see the boy's red-rimmed eyes filming over.

The old man said desperately, "Bill, the gold, the gold you got, son, where was that? Where was it, boy?"

Bill Jones turned his face away. The black tip of his tongue protruded between his teeth. His body strained to move, as if he wrestled some enormous unseen opponent. He choked for breath, and a pink film of blood appeared at the corner of his mouth.

"All right, son," the old man said in resignation. "I won't trouble you no more."

He continued to grip the young man's shoulders and hold his body still. The black head dropped back and the knotted muscles relaxed.

"Go peaceful; don't be scared," the old man said. "It's just eternal rest, and that ain't a bad go, is it?"

Presently the old man stood up, rubbing his hands on his pants. He hobbled away, mumbling to himself, to tend to the burros. He dug out the saddlebags suddenly and poured out the gold to look at it once more.

"No Ghost Lode," he said. "Just a plain, damned, lost strike." The samples winked dully, enigmatically. "The richest strike in the world," the old man said bitterly. "Old Ben Sandy, with the richest strike in the world. I've got it right here in my hand and I don't know where it is." He put the gold away again, with a savage emphasis, and went on with his work.

He looked down at Bill Jones. The young face was no longer feverish. The skin was as yellow as wax. The bloodshot eyes were blank.

"Dead enough," the old man said. "Besides everything else, I've got to dig you a grave."

He closed the boy's eyes and crossed his hands over his chest. He checked for a pulse automatically, and he was astonished to find it running gently on.

He was still alive when evening came. If anything, he was a little stronger. It was a sure thing, the old man thought, that he couldn't get any weaker, not if he was going to insist on hanging on to life the way he was doing. The old man made his supper and fed Bill Jones again with broth and water, and changed the bandage on his wounds. While he was about it he undressed him and washed him down and wrapped him in blankets. Then he went through his clothes, in the hope that he might find some lead on the location of the strike. It would be enough, he thought, if he could get a general idea of where it was. He found a few nondescript personal belongings, a handsome silver watch, and a notebook.

The notebook contained a penciled test log, evidently a record of face sampling taken at the strike. The old man could read it clearly enough. It indicated a narrow outcrop, apparently without much lateral extension, but within its short confines immensely rich. The old man could almost visualize it. But there was nothing in the notebook that gave a hint of its location.

He sat for a long while in thought. He got the bags of samples and took them close to the fire and gazed at them by the hour, as if they might sooner or later speak to him and tell him where they came from. At last he went to sleep.

In the morning Bill Jones was asking for water.

The old man hustled to him, half awake, with a drink. He said, "Bill, can you hear me? Can you hear me, son?"

The wounded man sipped at the water and laboriously swallowed.

"Look at me, son. Look here. Look at me. Can you hear what I'm saying?"

The young man's eyes opened and moved with an infinite effort. The old man's heart pounded with excitement.

"That gold, son, that ore you was carrying." The old man stopped to lick his lips and get his breath. The boy was looking at him, he understood him, he thought; he was going to be able to talk. "Can you remember where you found it? The gold. That gold."

Bill Jones moved his lips.

The old man gave him another taste of water. "Do you

144

remember, boy? Do you remember where you got it?"

Bill Jones tried to speak. The old man waited breathlessly.

Bill Jones said clearly enough, "I don't know."

"Of course you know!" the old man exploded. "You had it on you, boy!" The old man restrained his impatience. "I'm talking about those samples, son. Where'd they come from? Where was it?"

The old man waited, gripping his trembling hands together.

Bill Jones said in a dry whisper, "Don't know."

"You picked 'em up, didn't you?"

"Don't know. Don't know where it came from."

"You got to know! Would you lay there on your deathbed and lie to me?"

Bill Jones closed his eyes and seemed to sleep. The old man reached out to shake him awake, but the eyes would not open.

"You can't take a gold mine with you when you're dead, can you?" the old man demanded, enraged. "Listen, boy; listen to me. Wake up and listen to me."

Bill Jones slept on. The old man got up and stomped across the camp. He saw the watch and the notebook. He sat down and took the watch apart to make sure no clue was hidden within it. He leafed furiously through the notebook.

He yelled at the wounded man, "A dozen words, that's all I wanted! So you give me a lie!"

He got up and flung the notebook away, and a blue

quail, pecking at the ashes of the fire, scampered off, calling shrilly, "Queet, queet, queet!"

The old man shouted after it, "Run, blame you!"

He was struck by a sudden shift of thought.

These quail always ran. You could trot after one and shoot at him ten times and he wouldn't fly. They stayed on the ground because in this remote country they didn't know about hunters and guns. The killers they knew were hawks, which came from above and from which they customarily hid on the ground. When, rarely, you found quail that flushed, it usually meant the country had been recently hunted. When they were hunted enough they got in the habit of taking to wing. They learned, after a while, that running was not good enough to get away from a gun.

But the quail on the mesa had flushed.

"Why, that's it," the old man thought, in such excitement that he could not speak. "That's it, sure."

He was immediately certain that someone had been camped on the mesa lately and had killed the birds there regularly, day after day. He was as sure of it as if the birds themselves had told him.

And there was the arroyo, where the earth was split open, revealing a cross section of ancient benches and river-beds and decayed rock, that was where they would have been prospecting from a camp on the mesa. It all fit together. The strike was bound to be some place along the arroyo.

The old man bawled at the burros in a great voice, "Boys, I've got it!" Hasdrubal gave him a skeptical look.

The old man whooped at him, "It's enough to go on, ain't it? You bet your boots it is! Hellsfire, I'll walk right dab to it!"

He started away with the burros, scarcely aware that he had packed them. He ran back to the camp for the two bags of samples.

He howled at the sleeping Bill Jones, "Sure, keep it to yourself, son! Old Dad ain't as dumb as you thought!"

He was filled with derision for the pitiful, greedy efforts the wounded boy had made to conceal his treasure. Did he think he could show Ben Sandy ore like that and keep him from smelling out where it came from?

The old man laughed and hugged Hasdrubal round the neck as he stumped along.

He said, "Would of been a sight better of him to of told me, wouldn't it? All I done for him, and then he'd lie and try to cheat me! We got around him, didn't we? Didn't we, boys?"

The burros slanted their ears at him, and jogged on in their quick and dainty walk.

On the mesa the quail flew up and sailed away as before, and the old man shouted with glee to see them. He promised himself that he would buy the mesa and fence it in and feed these birds forever at his own expense.

He had thought he would push on straight to the wash, but when he reached the country rock of the arroyo rim he decided to make camp there, for the first thing. His legs were uncommonly tired. They trembled at each step. He would set up camp here, and then go to the wash and prospect up this far and be all set to turn in when he got here.

There was no point in looking for the site of Bill Jones's camp or the body of his partner. What with lions and coyotes and buzzards the dead partner could easily be scattered over half the mesa by now. He might find their workings or markers in the arroyo, and he might not. The thing to do was work the whole arroyo, prospect the float and the open bedrock, and before too many days he'd be sure to hit the spot. There was plenty of time, now that he was certain the strike was some place along here.

He clambered down the arroyo wall to a hardpan bench and crouched there and got his breath.

There was a delicious sense of anticipation that made him almost want to prolong the actual work of discovery. He took out the gold and looked at it, and time passed while he waited, unmoving, in a madness of inactivity. He laughed aloud at every plumed quail that whirred into the air above the poppies. He stood up at last, but his legs still shivered like stems of grass.

He laughed again and sat down on the bench, suddenly yawning. He hadn't rested long enough. But his legs continued to tremble even though they were stretched out at ease, and he could no longer hide from the truth. It was not weariness, but fear.

The boy's fever had gone this morning. Chances were, if he had pulled through this far, that he might live. That was part of the fear.

"He ain't got a chance of living," the old man said contemptuously, but he did not convince himself. "All right!" he said furiously. "If he lives, what happens to me? I let him go on and claim the whole thing and hog it for himself, do I?"

That was a still greater part of the fear, and he felt a hundred times better for having spoken it straight out. He looked around boldly at the silent rocks and the silent, brilliant flowers.

"Is there any laws says I'm bound to go on taking care of him?"

He remembered then that he had not even left water beside Bill Jones.

Was that murder? Had it been in his mind all day that he would commit murder for the strike he now knew he could find? Had he intended deliberately to leave the boy to die? He told himself he hadn't thought of Bill Jones at all, but the back of his mind, which had been thinking secretly of little else, told him coldly that was a lie.

Murder, and that was, at last, the whole fear.

The old man said plaintively, "Suppose I go back and take care of him and he pulls through? What do I get for it? He's made it plain enough what I'll get from him—not a thing. So what do I owe him?"

He poured out the ore samples and lifted them in his hands. They called to him with the deep, glorious music of their color. They enveloped his senses, they offered a vision of a cool, desirable world in payment for all the burned-out years of his life.

The boy would die easily. He was weak enough already; he would die as easily as going to sleep. That thread of pulse would quit, that was all. It might be stopping at this instant.

Why should he keep Bill Jones alive and let Bill Jones take the strike from him?

The old man jumped to his feet and threw the samples out into the arroyo. He grabbed up the rest of them from the ground and hurled them away with all his might. They rattled against the rocks and brush like so many common pebbles. He made his way back up to the mesa. He said to the burros, "Come on, boys. Bill Jones will be wanting a drink."

The burros moved off, and then stopped in their tracks, and the old man saw a brown-haired girl in a gingham dress coming toward him through the flowers.

She stopped and looked at him with a sweet, grave smile. She said, "Ben, think of this grass. You're such a fool sometimes."

The old man looked at the poppies and the grass under his feet, and a quail flew up, madly beating his way free of a snarl of grass. The poppies were a little jungle of feathery stems and the clumps of panic grass were each a tangled mat.

His eyes had been full of gold and he hadn't thought of the grass. He had dreamed that the flying quail meant there had been a camp here, because he had been thinking of nothing but the gold and some way of finding it. But it was the grass and the poppies, of course, that forced the quail to fly. They couldn't run through this thickly grown stuff. There had not been a prospector's camp on the mesa. There was no more reason, now, to think the lode was located in the arroyo. He had been wrong.

The girl was gone. A breeze swept across the mesa and the poppies bent before it, and the old man thought suddenly of the Ghost Lode. Throughout the day the Ghost Lode had been shut away from his mind as if by magic. He was stricken with a startling feeling of dread at the memory of how near he had been to murder. He moved on, hurrying the burros along.

Bill Jones was still sleeping when the old man reached the camp. He slept solidly through the night, and in the morning woke up feeling stronger and hungry, and able to talk.

His name, it happened, was not Bill Jones, which was neither here nor there to the old man; he would be Bill Jones to him for good. He was a college student. He had been spending his spring vacation on the Daly ranch the other side of the mountains, and he had taken a couple of horses and packed across the mountains to see the area.

In the mountains he had come upon a prospector who had apparently been injured in a fall. The man had broken his back and was paralyzed from the waist down. He was more dead than alive. He had said nothing, except to sing endlessly the song about Old Bill Jones. He had been carrying the two bags of ore samples and the notebook.

In a fit of delirium he became suspicious, seemed to fear that he was going to be robbed, and got hold of a gun and went to blazing away with it. Bill Jones tried to take the gun from him, and the prospector died of the effort of the fight. But during the struggle he shot Bill Jones through the body. Later, the boy's animals got away from him, and after that he didn't know anything that happened until he came to in the old man's camp. He guessed he had tried to walk, and he had naturally gone the easiest way, downhill, which had led him to the desert.

"Ghost Lode," the old man said.

"I brought his gold with me," Bill Jones said. "You can have it if you want it. If you ask me, I'd say it's got a curse on it." He grinned diffidently. "I've been having the damn'dest dreams about it."

"I know," the old man said.

"It weighed me down," Bill Jones explained, as if it was necessary to make the dream absolutely clear. "It piled up on me, like I was dead and buried. Seemed like it was there for a week so I couldn't hardly breathe, but now it's gone."

"I know," the old man said.

THE MAN AT GANTT'S PLACE

By Steve Frazee

THE MAN AT GANTT'S PLACE is a top-level description of the growing-up of a kid in the Old West—the gunplay and other occurrences which turn his footsteps in the right direction.

WITH the time at hand for the actual break, Lew Gantt was a little nervous. He did not return to the wild-horse corral after dinner to continue replacing posts that old Stump had chalked as unsound. Work was all there ever had been around this place—fix something before it busted, get ready for winter, get ready for summer, scatter grass seed from heck to breakfast, push yourself into old age by trying to look ahead so blamed far.

Lew was seventeen and one day. He had waited the one day so Stump could not say it was because of his birthday. He went down to where Stump was watching Railroad Costigan lead a big, wall-eyed bay gelding around the breaking corral.

Stump did not ask why Lew was loafing. He did not even look at his son, and that made Lew more uneasy. Old

Stump just stood there watching Railroad and the bay, and after a while he said. "Try a blanket on him, Railroad."

The gelding did not like the blanket, and Costigan had a devil of a time. The way to break horses was to top 'em off and show 'em who was boss, and get things done without a lot of fooling around. But no, Lew's father would rather get six mounts half gentled in two weeks than break a whole corralful in a week; he did everything that way.

Old Stump had just been too long up here in the hills, looking down at Revelation Valley, where they did things with a bang. He was pretty old, all right—anyway past forty, Lew figured. He studied his father from the side. Not a very big man at all, but he was pretty tightly put together. He didn't care much what he wore, even a patch on the seat of his pants. His mouth was sort of tight, and he did not use it much. He shaved every morning. He never leaned or sprawled all over things, like Lew was doing right now. He favored a bench to sit on, or a stool. Chairs with backs made men without backbones, Stump always said.

Lew knew plenty about his father, and none of it was very interesting. Lew put both feet on the ground.

"Work him until he'll carry the blanket," Stump said. "Don't rush him. There's going to be a good saddle horse."

Don't rush nothing! Stump had been here when he could have taken up the choice part of Revelation Valley, where the Mexican Spur had its home ranch now; but no, he had to settle up here in the dry hills where there was water one year and not much the next year. He let the cattlemen run over him, even let them range some of their stuff up here without saying boo about it. If he saw a critter that was loaded up on larkspur, down and bloated and dying, he took his knife and tried to save it. Generally he never even bothered to tell anyone.

"What is it, Lew?"

"Uh—I—" The old man was looking at him like he knew just what Lew was thinking. Aw, it was just that slow way of his when he threw a study on anything. "I'm leaving, Stump. I got to do something besides fix fences and make little dams and fool around with horses, and besides . . ." Lew let it drift away like smoke.

Stump never let anything drift. "Besides what?"

You couldn't tell old Stump about things he had never felt, of the wishing rock in the pines where Lew sat sometimes at night, looking at the twinkling pinpoints in the valley, wondering what everybody was doing down there; about his clothes and the beat-up wagon when he went to Revelation for supplies, and saw the cowboys thundering down the street, yelling and shooting, plunging off their horses in front of the Valley Saloon; about the time the four fancy women from Arbor's Dance Hall passed Lew on the street, looking at him with the merest brush of interest that died before it really lived, telling him that they figured him in a class with the nesters from the range east of town. Stump wouldn't understand those things at all.

"I'm riding out," Lew said.

Stump put out his hand. "So long, son." They shook hands, and Stump turned back to the corral.

Lew spun away and went to the house. Lew's mother was sitting in the big rocker with brass-capped arms, looking out the bay window at Gantt Creek and the pines with sunlight on them. She wasn't much for sitting around. Nobody who stayed around old Stump did much sitting, Lew thought bitterly, except Odalie, and she was only a brat sister. He heard Marian in the kitchen.

"I'm leaving, Ma," Lew said.

Mrs. Gantt did not seem surprised, and that nettled Lew a little. "Where are you going?"

"Down in the valley for a spell. If I don't like it there, maybe I'll drift on west a few hundred miles." He had not intended to add the last, because his vague plans extended no farther than the valley, but now that it was out, it sounded pretty good. Some of the riders who brought horses up to Stump had told Lew of far places that old Stump didn't even know about. Why, out there on those distant ranges, where a man wasn't known just as Stump Gantt's boy. . . .

"We packed your things, son."

Lew blinked. Marian came on into the living room with a sort of scared smile on her face. Anyway, there was one person around here who thought it was bad that he was going so far away. Marian was a pretty girl, with her mother's slenderness and dark good looks, but she was just another sister.

"Well, I'm going," Lew said. He wanted to tell his mother how crazy it was for all of them to stay up here in the hills and work themselves old for Stump. But his mother did not look so old right then. In fact, she did not look a heck of a lot older than Marian. She sure was a healthy, strong woman, to look so good after putting up with old Stump all these years.

"I guess I'll get my stuff." Lew went upstairs to his room. Odalie was there, her face buried so deeply into his pillow that only her red pigtails showed. "What the devil are you—" She raised her head and he saw that she was crying, so instead of finishing by asking what she was doing in his room, he said "—bawling about, Odalie?"

"You're going away!" she wailed.

"Well, cut it out. I'm only going a couple thousand miles, and maybe in a few years I'll come back."

"A few years!" Odalie began to wail louder.

"I'll bring you back something."

Odalie rolled over and looked at him. She sniffed a little. "What?"

"A parasol."

"I want a saddle."

Lew considered. He probably would be in the chips when he returned. . . .

Odalie saw his hesitation, and began to screw up her face.

"All right!" he said. "A saddle."

"With silver trimmings?"

"I make no promises about that."

Odalie began to laugh. "You look just like Pa when he says that!" She wiped at her tears with the bends of her wrists, then laughed some more.

She sure was a pug-nosed, scheming little brat. Lew scowled at her, and then he grinned. "Where's my war-bag?"

"It's in there." Odalie pointed at a flat leather bag lying on a chair. "So's your noisy old six-gun that Pa wouldn't let you wear."

Lew looked disgustedly at the bag. "That thing!"

"Ma says that folks who carry their belongings in war-bags don't know where they're going. She says—"

"I know what she says. I know what everybody around here says! That's why I'm going away for keeps."

"You said you'd be back, with my saddle—with the silver trimming."

Lew shook his head. Sisters, parents—they gave you nothing but arguments. Odalie trailed him downstairs. Marian was standing by Mrs. Gantt, and Marian was getting ready to bawl. Lew gave them each an awkward hug. He would have hugged Odalie, but she made a face at him and ran out the back door.

Mrs. Gantt looked at Lew the way she had when he was a little boy. "Stay decent, stay clean, Lew." She looked at him a moment longer and then started toward the kitchen. "Come on, Marian. Let's finish the dishes."

Lew threw his sprung saddle on old, rough-coated, slow Ranger, the only horse he had ever owned. Stump did not even look away from the breaking corral when Lew rode past, but Railroad stared at the black bag behind the saddle, and then went over to the bars and asked Stump something.

"He's going out to try on a new pair of britches,"

Stump said. "Put the saddle on the gelding now, Railroad."

"Good luck, Lew!" Railroad called.

Lew waved. Over in the pines Odalie was jumping up and down on the wishing rock, yelling his name. He waved at her, then turned toward the valley.

Mrs. Gantt and Marian cleaned up the dishes in silence, then Mrs. Gantt went to the back door and called Odalie in from the wishing rock.

"Go down the trail after Lew, Odie. When you get near the gyp rock caves, watch Ranger's tracks carefully until—"

"I know, Ma! He'll stop and switch his plunder from that suitcase into his dirty old warbag, and hide the suitcase in one of the caves."

Mrs. Gantt smiled on the thin line between laughter and tears. "Bring the suitcase back, Odie."

Marian said, "At least, he didn't ride away looking like a saddle bum, even if nobody but us saw him."

Down at the corral, Stump's brown, clean-shaved face showed no change, except that his mouth was a little tighter. From the corner of his eye he saw Odalie running down the trail, but mainly he watched the baby gelding circling nervously with the saddle on its back.

"Ride him, Railroad."

Slim and wiry, Costigan stopped in mid-stride. "What?"

"I said ride him!"

Railroad's eyes went sidewise, toward the valley.

"You don't mean that, Stump."

"No, I guess I don't." Stump Gantt walked away toward the upper meadow.

Railroad called after him, "Never was a kid that was any good didn't pull his picket pin a few times!"

Gantt went on walking. Railroad resumed his patient circling of the corral, now and then speaking to the bay in a soothing voice, and all the time thinking of the days when he was seventeen down in Arizona Territory, many years before. He made a dozen trips around the big corral before he noticed the gelding was no longer humping or pulling sidewise in an effort to get from under leather.

Railroad stopped then, facing the emerald flatness of the distant valley, looking far beyond the purple ranges. He was glad that his guns had long ago been laid aside. Here was the only place he had ever been at home, at peace. If he were seventeen again . . . if he were seventeen and knew what he knew now . . . life would be awful dull.

Free with fifty dollars in his pocket, Lew strolled the main street of Revelation. Now that he was here, all the things he had longed to do when he was not free to do them did not have the same appeal. He would be a little cautious about what he did first, sort of get the feel of things. There was no rush.

He saw Mexican Spur horses in front of the Valley Saloon, and four or five Short Fork horses before the Green Grass Saloon. There was not a single nester wagon in town. It was time the danged nesters learned they couldn't move right in on cattle range. They claimed to have legal right, but Lew did not take much stock in that; in fact, he knew only the superficial facts about the trouble that was shaping up, but his sympathy was with the cowmen, so he did not need to have many facts.

Gaunt, blistered Custer Wigram, owner of the Spur, came from the Valley as Lew was passing for the third time. He bunched pale brows at Lew and said, "Howdy, kid. What's Stump doing in town in the middle of the week?"

"He ain't here, Mr. Wigram."

Wigram sized the youth up once more. Lew's levi's were new, but he had soaked them for a week in mild lye water to take away their giveaway blueness. He was wearing the long barreled .44, for which he had traded a month's work at Wigram's hay ranch the year before.

"Oh," Wigram said in a long breath. "You're out on your own now, huh?"

"Yeah."

Townspeople passed. Four cowboys drifted from the Green Grass to the Valley. They all spoke with deference to Wigram. Lew did not mind at all being seen talking on equal terms to the biggest rancher in the country.

"How does it look out there?" Lew nodded east.

Wigram shook his head. "We overlooked a thing or two when we settled here. Then we didn't work together." His eyes strayed toward the west hills. "A few days ago four farmers filed on the very ground Joe Hemphill's home ranch stands on."

Hemphill owned the Short Fork. Lew cursed to show

concern. Not used to profanity, he overdid it. "That won't stand, will it?"

"I don't know." Wigram shook his head dubiously.

"You ought to run every nester out of the country right damn now!"

The Spur owner smiled vaguely. "That would be quite a drive—now. You want a job, Lew?"

Lew's heart leaped. Never be overanxious, Stump always said. "Well . . . my horse ain't too good with cows."

"All you'll need him for is to ride to Spur. I want some range stuff broke."

That was a wet slap. Break horses! There was no fun in that, not doing it Stump's slow way, which was the only method Lew understood.

"Your old man says you're about as good as Costigan."

"Huh!" Stump had never mentioned that to Lew.

"No, thanks, Mr. Wigram. I don't much care for that kind of work."

The corners of Wigram's eyes crinkled. "Too much like home, huh?" Then he started up the walk. "Ride over if you change your mind."

The youth swung his gun belt around and went into the Valley. Spur and Short Fork riders at the bar were talking about the nesters. There was a pause until Shindy Lemons said, "Aw, that's only Stump Gantt's boy from the west hills. C'mon over, Lew, and have a drink."

Lew was awkward at the bar, not sure just what to do with his hands. He saw the others watching him closely, and knew they were guessing it was his first drink of whiskey. It was. No rush about it. He took his time.

"Hmm!" a cowboy said. "Old Stump must run a still up there."

They all laughed. Lew tossed a coin on the bar. "Have one around on me." It was the thing to do, but he sure didn't like to see the money go into the till. There were better ways to spend money, and while the whiskey was loosening social tightness inside him, he still didn't think it was worth good gold that he had been a long time saving. He had a drink on four others, and he could honestly say that, other than a sort of warm pushing behind his eyes, the whiskey did not seem to affect him.

Before it was his turn to buy again, he thanked the cowboys and strolled over to a poker game in the corner. Confidential Pete, the houseman, was having a bad time with Buck Hodel, the Spur foreman, and a slim stranger dressed in gray. Ivers, the liveryman, and two cowboys were in the game, too.

"Jump in, kid, and get your feet wet," Hodel said. He was a broad, black-browed man, about half drunk at the moment. He had a pretty bad temper, they said.

"No rush," Lew said. "I like to see where the power is before I jump."

"You sound just like your old man," Hodel said.

The stranger in gray smiled at Lew. It was hard to figure that one out. He was a handsome devil, gray eyes, curly brown hair and a clean grin. His face was brown and so were his hands, and he wasn't dressed quite like a gambler, not the kind old Railroad talked about, leastwise. But he was dressed just a little better than a range hand, too.

Lew watched the game. One of the cowboys won a small pot. The stranger won a big one when the houseman bucked into a full house with two pair. After a while Lew got things figured out. The man in gray was merely having a big lucky streak, and the others were letting him draw too cheap when they should have been raising the devil.

At least, that was the way Railroad Costigan would have figured it, and Lew had spent many an evening playing poker for fun with Railroad.

This beat drinking whiskey. Lew itched to get into the game, but he waited a while, watching how they played, before he bought forty dollars' worth of chips.

Confidential Pete hesitated before he shoved the stack across. "You sure you know how to play this, Gantt?"

"I learn fast."

Pete grunted, "I don't want your old man on my neck after you lose your money." He was half afraid it was Stump's money.

Lew grinned. "Worry about the man who owns this dump getting on *your* neck after I take *his* money."

The stranger laughed. "You'll do, Gantt. Smoky Cameron." He put out his hand as Lew settled into a chair beside him.

"Lew Gantt." The name had a fair sound, at that. Cameron's hand was hard, with work bumps there, all right, but not the dry-raspy kind. He had not worked recently, Lew figured.

Lew drifted along for about a half hour, like someone who wanted to make his forty bucks last a long time. And then on a pot that Hodel opened for five dollars, five men stayed. Lew was the last one. He raised five. One of the cowboys dropped out. Everybody else stayed. They drew cards. Ivers took one. He cursed. Before he tossed in his hand he spread it to show how he had missed a flush. Nobody paid any attention. They were all watching Lew, who had not drawn any cards.

"Beginner's luck!" one of the cowboys muttered, and threw away his hand.

Hodel bet five dollars, scowling at Lew. The houseman stayed, and raised five more. When it came to Lew he met the raise and pushed in all the chips he had.

"Never try to bluff a dumb kid," Pete said. He tossed his hand away.

Cameron got out with a laugh, and that left it up to Hodel. He scowled and grunted and tried to read Lew's face, and at last threw his hand away with a curse. "What have you got you're so proud of?"

Lew pushed his hand into the discards. "You didn't pay to see, Hodel." Lew had been bluffing.

"I think he was pulling a whizzer," Cameron said good-humoredly.

"He's too dumb for that!" Hodel growled. But still he was not sure. It showed in his eyes, and it would keep eating at him. The next time he would call anything, Lew figured. And that was just what happened an hour later.

Hodel was still far ahead of the game, and Lew had made steady little winnings, so he now had about two hundred dollars.

He got a full house, queens over sixes, on the deal. When the smoke cleared there was about two hundred dollars in the pot, with only Lew and Hodel left. The Spur foreman had drawn one card, and Lew was sure he had filled something. Hodel pushed out chips to match everything Lew had. His face went splotchy red when he saw the full house. He slapped a Jack-high straight on the cloth and pushed his chair back savagely.

"You're just too damned lucky, Gantt, or else—"

"Else what?"

"—or you're too slick for this game. You'd better get out now."

Cameron said, "Don't push on the lines, Hodel. The kid's been lucky, and played good poker."

Hodel's face swung like a club at Cameron. "You keep that little thing under your nose quiet, tinhorn. I ain't just sure about you anyway."

"Is that a fact?" Cameron rose. "Just what is it you aren't sure about?"

Lew had his chance to get from under, but he wasn't letting anyone carry the load for him. "It's a free country, Hodel. Get out yourself if you don't like the way I play." An instant later he thought that maybe the whiskey had not been quite as harmless as it seemed.

"Why, you little west-hills pup!" Hodel kicked his chair away. He was a blocky, solid man, and it was his boast that he could lick any man in the valley.

Confidential Pete's voice was a lost squeal. "No trouble in here, boys! No trouble in here!"

Across the room a Spur rider said to the bartender, "No, Sammy. Just lay your little white mitts on the cherrywood and watch the fun."

"I guess," Hodel said, "I'd better slap some manners into you, Gantt." He flung aside a cowboy who was struggling to rise with his feet entangled in the baling-wire braces of his chair. Hodel walked through the space toward Lew.

Lew went around the table. He was hot-scared, but he was not going to run.

"Stay back, Hodel," he said.

The Spur foreman made a lunge. Lew kicked a chair in front of him and went farther around the table. Hodel crashed over the chair and fell. He came up insane with anger.

"Stay back, Hodel." Lew kept the table between them. He saw it coming then. He could almost smell the brimstone scent of it.

Hodel went for his pistol.

He was not fast. No one in the Revelation country was fast with a gun. Lightning draws were merely something men like Railroad talked about. But Buck Hodel was faster than Lew Gantt, who had never drawn his .44 quickly, except in secret practice against old Railroad.

The explosion almost deafened Lew. He did not hear or feel the bullet, and he did not know where it went until someone told him afterward. He smelled the great bloom of dirty-gray powder smoke that obscured the middle of

Hodel's body. Lew had drawn by then, and now he shot, trying to aim through the rising murk and hit Hodel in the right leg to knock him flat. Instead, he shot Hodel through the side. The man twisted back and fell into the check rack.

Lew had to step to one side to see through the acrid fumes. Hodel was lying there, his mouth open with shock. Lew Gantt stared. He was scared to death, and sick.

Smoky Cameron was against the wall, off to one side. His gun was in his hand and his eyes were on the Spur and Short Fork men. "Was it fair?" he asked.

After a moment grizzled Rip Goodwin said, "Yeah, it was fair." He sent a sullen, wicked look at Lew. The cowboys went over to Hodel.

With his gun still in his hand, Lew started to run. He would get Ranger. He would ride as fast as he could, clear out of the country. He had killed a man, and a deadly fear was riding him and urging him to get away quickly.

Cameron caught him at the door. Lew clubbed his gun and tried wildly to beat the man away, but Cameron caught his wrist and hurled him against the wall.

"Where you going, Gantt?"

After a while Lew stopped struggling. He stared at Cameron. The man was calm and friendly. "I know," Cameron said. "You want to run from here to the Pacific. I know how you feel. Put that gun away and sit down there in a chair."

Lew obeyed, gaining control from Cameron's quiet voice. The man in gray went back to the poker table. He scooped Lew's chips into his hat. He stood there a while looking steadily at Confidential Pete, and after a few moments Pete took his hand from his coat pocket and added a fistful of yellow chips to the hat. Cameron found two more in the pocket.

"Them are mine!" Pete protested. Cameron dropped the chips in the hat.

"Interest on a filthy trick," he said. Pete slunk away.

About then Lew heard Hodel curse weakly and say something to Goodwin. A breath of terror went out of Lew.

The sheriff came in with Plug Riddle, the druggist, who was also the doctor for men and horses. A lot of people streamed in, crowding close to Hodel, then turning to stare in surprise at the boy in the chair by the door.

Riddle said loudly. "If he don't get complications or something, he may be all right in a month or so."

Lew stood up, and his legs held him without shaking. He wanted to tell Hodel he was sorry, but just then Wigram came over, a savage, calculating look on his face. "For a punk button, you sure messed things up, didn't you?"

"He started it."

Wigram turned away and went to the bar. Cameron came up and handed Lew a canvas sack. "Five hundred and twenty-five."

Lew wanted to throw the gold through the window. He wished he had never left home. No matter whose fault this was, it made him sick again to see blood dripping as they carried Hodel out.

Sheriff Nate Springer was a big, slow-moving, chunky man who surveyed everything thoughtfully from green eyes almost buried under his brows. Stump said he got that way from figuring how to stay in office the rest of his life.

"I don't figure to make a fuss," the sheriff told Lew, "but you better come down to the office with me."

Wigram turned around at the bar. "Let's hear what you got to say right here, Springer."

"He said his office." Cameron took Lew's arm and hustled him outside, and a moment later Springer followed, relieved because he had not been forced to argue the matter.

They did not go inside. Springer kept his office neat, and he did not like dirt on the oiled floor or things moved out of place on his desk.

Springer said. "You'd best get on back home right away, Gantt—and stay clear of town for quite a spell."

"What for? I didn't start anything."

"I don't like trouble here."

"It wasn't my fault!" Lew said.

"Nobody said it was. Go on home."

"You want to run me out of town just because I'm only a kid, but you don't say nothing about running the others out because Spur and Fork elect you."

Springer nodded slowly. "That's right as far as it goes. Also, I don't want to have more grief when some drunk cowboy sees you around and jumps you."

"I'll take care of myself."

"That's what I'm afraid of," Springer said quietly.

"Stump Gantt's likely to have enough trouble on his hands, without his son trying to be a gun fighter."

"I don't want to be a gun fighter, and I didn't start anything, so I don't see what right you got to tell me to beat it."

The sheriff looked at Cameron. "It's still the best thing for you, kid."

That was what Lew was mainly tired of, someone telling him what he ought to do.

"You ordering me to go?" he asked.

"No, but I sure suggest it strong." Springer sighed. He turned away and went into his office.

"I wasn't figuring to stay anyway," Lew said to Cameron. "Now I might."

Cameron asked casually. "What are you planning to do with the money?" Lew was still holding the sack.

"Half of it is yours. If you hadn't picked the chips up, I wouldn't have any money at all. And I think you had me beat that first hand I won, when I shoved in everything I had."

"Yes," Cameron said, "I knew you were bluffing." He smiled briefly. "It would have saved a lot of trouble if I'd busted you right there."

"Yeah," Lew said, thinking of the way Hodel had looked on the dirty floor. "I don't much care about this money now."

"I'll be glad to ease half of your conscience."

They went behind the livery stable to divide the gold.

"You drifting out?" Lew asked. He'd go along with Cameron if Cameron asked him. "You won't stand much chance to get a job here now—after siding in with me today."

"You may be right," Cameron said vaguely. "But I thought I'd look the ranches over and see what I could stir up. I sort of like this country."

"Huh! It ain't much."

Cameron gave him a grave look. "Maybe you've lived too close to it to see its good points, Lew."

A short time later Lew watched Cameron ride away on a leggy claybank that was a jim-dandy. Lew thought of old Ranger there in the stable. He had enough money now to make a trade for a good horse, but he hated to part with Ranger. No need to rush things. Maybe later, when Cameron returned from looking for a job nobody would give him, the two of them could ride away together.

Lew put a hundred dollars in the bank. He did not know just why he did, unless it was because Stump was always saying a man ought to save something out of every chunk he made. The banker was glad to take the money. He asked a lot of questions about how Stump was, and you'd have thought old Stump was a big wheel around the valley.

In two days the draw game in the Green Grass took everything Lew had in his pockets. He walked past the bank several times before he went in to get his hundred dollars. The banker was just as polite as before.

When Lew went out the nesters were coming into town. There was quite a bunch of them. Judging from the rifles and shotguns on their wagon seats, a man could say they were ready for trouble if it came.

Lew studied the farmers pretty closely. They were clean, quiet, going about their business as if they figured to be in the country a long time. A few days in Revelation taught Lew that the town was not against the nesters. Maybe the farmers did have some right on their side.

A nester named Cranklow, a raw-boned, sun-blistered man with a square jaw, said hello to Lew, and the youth remembered him from the times Cranklow had been to the horse ranch to talk to Stump about grass seed and dams. Cranklow stopped to talk, but Lew just said hello curtly and went on toward the Green Grass.

Lew was pretty lonely right then, and it occurred to him how he would have felt if someone had been short with him for no reason. A lot of people had talked to Lew, but generally only to ask how he had become so fast with a pistol.

He was cleaned out in three hours, losing his last twenty dollars when he tried to run a busted flush past the house-man's two pairs. He was hungry when he reached the street. At noon he had eaten well, but now, knowing he was broke, he was hungry ahead of time. He stood there wondering what his mother would have for supper that night.

Three cowboys from two-bit outfits were lounging at the hitch rail, watching the farmers leaving town in a body.

The devil could take the whole works, he thought angrily. He did not want anything to do with nesters, and cattlemen wanted nothing to do with him since he shot Buck Hodel. The thing to do was get as far away as possible from this two-bit valley and find a good riding job where nobody knew he was Stump Gantt's kid from the west hills, or that he had shot a man. Something deep inside him warned him that he was not thinking straight, but he was too flushed with resentment to pay any attention.

To heck with Smoky Cameron, too. Cameron had taken half of the five hundred and not even asked Lew to ride out with him. Lew Gantt was on his own. He did not owe anyone anything. He could do as he pleased. He was. . . .

Pitching hay at a nester place two days later for a dollar a day and all he could eat. The whole deal had been Cameron's idea, after he returned from riding the ranches and reported no jobs available. Cameron was pitching hay right alongside Lew. The weather held good. For a month they moved from place to place. Lew kept his eyes open and learned a lot.

The last place was Jemmie Cranklow's, on Little Elk, smack in the middle of what had been Spur range. Cranklow had put in a pile of work. He was figuring on planting winter wheat, and building a canal to water his upper eighty.

"This is as good farmland as any in the valley." Cameron explained. "It's even more sheltered." He put up a shock of hay to Cranklow's youngest boy on the rack. "The thing is, these people have made legal filings. Some of the ranchers don't even own the land where their buildings are. Wigram got wise two years ago and protected himself, but Hemphill waited too long. Now he'll have to compromise or lose the very land he lives on."

Lew looked sidewise at Cameron's gray clothes. "You know quite a bit about this valley, don't you?"

"I do." Cameron hoisted a shock that made the fork handle creak. "You favor law, don't you?"

"I guess I do. What happens, though, if there's a big fight?"

"There won't be," Cameron said. "Not on this side of the valley. The farmers are too strong here now."

Lew couldn't seem to get his fork into shocks just right for a long time. Stump had been throwing grass seed around in the west hills since before Lew—or even Marian —was born. He owned rock claims, timber claims, placers, five homesteads that had fizzled—just about everything that was worth a dime over there. Come to think of it, Stump had been building something slowly in the west hills. A man could run cattle there now, not like it used to be on this side, of course, but still the west hills would stand grazing. Spur and Short Fork were already running stuff over there.

The cowmen were beat on this side, but over there— just one man standing between them and all the range.

"My father has got legal claim to everything he holds!" Lew said.

"I know. So have the farmers over this way."

Sheriff Springer had it figured out. That's what he had meant when he said Stump was going to have trouble.

Wigram said he had overlooked something, and then he had glanced toward the west hills.

"I was at your father's place after I left Revelation," Cameron said casually. "I never saw so much good solid craftsmanship in everything around there."

"My father does things right!" Lew was darned sure of that now, having seen plenty of work that wasn't done well.

In the shadowy bunkhouse at Stump Gantt's horse ranch the owner and Railroad Costigan looked at each other past a dim lamp on the table between two Walker Colts that were shiny-worn.

Costigan's face was as brown and wrinkled as a frost-rotted apple. "They might be a little afraid of him, Stump. It wasn't luck when he shot Hodel. They might want him out of the way."

"Cameron's with him."

"Cameron has to go prowling at times."

Gantt shook his head. "He's on his own. It's got to be that way. We've got to let him make his own decisions, Railroad."

He shook his head sadly. "I never thought it would come down to this again. I guess I've just been blind to everything you've been doing here, Stump, scattering seed, making those little rock dams. . . . Of course, it's been only the last year or two that the results began to show up."

Stump nodded somberly. "They still call 'em the 'dry

hills,' but Wigram and Hemphill have seen, and Springer saw it long ago."

"Springer won't be no help."

Stump smiled. "When did we ever ask the law for help?"

"Maybe I'm getting old." Railroad said. "Maybe I've slipped since I been here, but it seems to me this is one time when the law ought to work. You've spent the best part of your life here, Stump, raising a family, building up a range that no one wanted, putting every dime into developing something. Now—"

"That makes it all the more worth fighting for. I didn't want the fight. I hoped they'd learn from what was happening over east, but now a fight is all that's left."

"Wigram is ordinarily a reasonable man." Railroad picked up the other gun. "Joe Hemphill isn't much on fighting."

"Wigram is desperate now. I offered to lease the west hills. I made him a good offer. Hodel was the one who made him stiffen when he was about to come around. Wigram knows he's been beat over east. He knows it too late, and it rankles all the more to think he let the west hills get away from him. He's carrying Hemphill, too. Joe don't want the fight. Joe was the one who stopped Wigram from burning out nesters years ago, when the cowmen might have made it stick.

"Now Wigram is working on Hemphill by telling him what a terrible mistake that was. They're both ruined unless they get the west hills, and Hemphill's ruined any way you figure it, because Wigram will ease him out later if they win. I've let them run a few cattle over here, Railroad. They let me take a beef whenever we needed meat. The hides have always been right there on the fence for anyone to see. I got the worst of it, of course, but I wanted to see just how well the west hills would stand up under grazing. They'll stand it, but we'll have to watch the dry years and cut herds—and there will never be a time when my range will stand one third of the cows Spur and Short Fork have."

Costigan picked up both guns. His eyes had a young look in his old, brown face. "A man never changes, Stump. I thought maybe you had, since the old days in Arizona, but you're just the same inside." He scowled. "How about Emily and the kids?"

"Emily got sore when I tried to edge around to sending her away. She knows what we both know, Railroad—nothing is any good to you unless you get it the hard way and hold it the same way against all comers."

Stump hesitated at the door, looking at the warm lights of the house. When Cameron, that young United States Marshal, had been here, he and Marian had looked at each other with the same expression springing in their eyes that Stump remembered from long ago, when he first saw Emily.

Stump looked toward the valley. It was overcast tonight, with a threat of rain, and the lights down there were not visible. Why didn't Lew come back? He must know by now how things were shaping up. But if he did not come back, he was still a boy that Stump Gantt was mighty proud of. Stump's mouth was sort of loose when he thought that perhaps he should have hinted that to Lew now and then, but such things came hard to Stump.

Stump's mouth was tight when he turned again toward the room. "You and me both know how easy it is to stop a fight before it gets started."

Railroad's eyes were wicked and narrow. Both Walkers were in holsters on his hips, and he was standing there with something on his mind that made him look as wound-up and dangerous as he had been in the old days. Stump and Railroad had ridden much of the West together as young men, and Railroad was the only man Stump had ever known who could actually use two guns with quick accuracy. There was a cold spot on Costigan's conscience; he had never worried about killing men who asked for it.

"Yeah," Railroad said. "Blast a rattler's head and all you got left is a lot of sickening twisting and humping. The trouble is all gone."

"Hodel is up and around," Stump said slowly. "He's been making talk about Lew, and about the west hills, too. It struck me that you might figure to go down and take Hodel and Wigram."

"Did it?" Railroad stood there, thin and wrinkled, wearing the tough, blank look Stump had almost forgotten.

"You wouldn't figure to come clear," Stump said. "You think you've lived a long time, but the older we get the better we like the thought of getting still older. We both want to live to see Lew running this place, see the girls

179

married off to decent youngsters, with you and me having time to fool around with blooded horses, like we've always wanted."

"Sure," Railroad said. "I've thought of all that. I've also thought that we ain't got much chance, waiting for them to come after us."

Stump had never been one to try to make words change facts. He said, "That's right. But we've got to stay with the law all the way. That's the way this place was built, and that's the way I want to leave it. We've got the right to defend ourselves, but we can't go out and start killing before we're attacked."

After a while the tenseness went out of Railroad. He sat down on a bench and he was just an old man wearing two pistols that were out of date. "I wish Lew would come back," he muttered.

"Maybe he will." Stump peered again at dark mist over the valley. He shut the door quietly and went toward the house. Before he crossed the flagstone porch he straightened his shoulders and composed his face, so Odalie, at least, would not know what he was thinking. With him and Railroad gone, Emily would still be in legal possession of most of the west hills. Wigram knew that, and he also knew that women could not run a horse ranch. After doing half his work by violence, Wigram would do the other half legally, letting shock and necessity wear Emily to the point of selling everything at his price.

It was worry about Lew that made Stump feel scared and helpless. They would figure to take Lew first. He went inside. Emily read his face, and then glanced toward

the bedroom where Marian was waging a battle to get
Odalie down for the night.

"Has the rain start—" Emily asked.

"Pa! Lew's going to bring me a silver-mounted saddle,
just my size, and a real Navajo bridle!" Odalie popped
out of the bedroom.

"Is that a fact?"

"It ought to be. I've told you about ten times," Odalie
said. "When's Lew coming back?"

"When he gets ready. Get to bed, Odie." Stump looked
at his wife. "It's fixing to rain, all right."

Blocking the bedroom door, Marian turned her head
to look at her parents. There was a starkness in the room
as the first drops began to fall.

In the mow of Cranklow's barn Lew shook hay from his
blankets and prepared to go to bed. "I'm going home
tomorrow," he told Cameron.

Standing by the ladder, fully dressed, Cameron was
silent as the rain hit the roof in a steady whisper. Then he
said. "It's too far now, Lew, too far across the valley and
up through the rocks to the west hills."

"I don't think I get you, Cameron."

"You wouldn't get there, Lew."

After a while Lew asked, "Wigram?"

"In a day or two I'll need your help. We can keep this
thing from ever starting, maybe. Will you stay with me,
Lew?"

"I don't know what you're going to do." Lew decided

he did not know much about Cameron at all. The man had a habit of riding out almost every night, and never saying where he went.

"Believe me, you can help your father more by staying with me and helping me than by getting waylaid on your way home."

"I'll stay two days."

"Wear your gun," Cameron said. He went down the ladder. Ten minutes later Lew heard him head the claybank toward Revelation.

The slender little man rode into the yard while Lew was still eating breakfast. The others had finished, but Lew was having one last stack of pancakes when he heard the man ask, "How do you get to Stump Gantt's place?"

Cameron's voice was casual. "How'd you happen to get so far north of the road, stranger?"

Lew took his gun belt off the peg by the wash bench and strapped it on before he went out. If the man looked at him at all it was merely a side flick of eyes like black chips. "I got off the track last night," the fellow said. "Where at is this Gantt place?"

"What do you want with Stump Gantt?" Cameron asked.

Whew! Cameron sure didn't mind asking personal questions.

The man didn't mind answering either. "That old cut-throat gave me a rasping on a horse I bought from him a few months back. I aim to get some satisfaction."

"You waited quite a while to squawk, didn't you?"

182

Cameron glanced at the man's mount, a deep-barreled bay with a beautiful saddle. "That the horse?"

"Yeah."

Lew was walking forward stiffly, so mad he could hardly see. "You're a dirty liar, mister," he said. "My father never cheated nobody in his life, and you're another dirty liar when you say that horse ever came from his place."

"Easy, Lew!" Cameron said.

It was too late. The man swung his face toward Lew, and the boy got his first full glimpse of the stranger. There was a deadly sort of blankness in the face, a frozen look of concentration in the black eyes. Lew realized he had stepped full-on into something pretty stout. It did not make any difference. Nobody was lying about old Stump while he was around.

"You call me a liar?" the man asked.

"Twice," Lew said. "What do you want to do about it?"

The man stretched thin lips across rows of teeth that were small and brown and strong. "You know I can't take that kind of talk, sonny."

Lew was not angry now. The thing fell into place in his mind. If he had used his head at all a minute before, he would have seen how raw and direct the whole plant was. He ought to back out right now. Native pride would not let him. He sensed that this little man would not make any of Buck Hodel's mistakes.

"Kid . . ." the man said casually, and went for his pistol. It was all too fast for Lew. He saw the fellow's gun come clear. He heard the ear-stunning roar, and saw the man spin clear around and almost fall. And then the stranger was standing there, gray-faced, his gun on the ground, his right arm hanging heavily, with blood sopping all around the elbow.

Cameron's pistol was in his hand, and a cloud of stinking, acrid smoke was drifting away from it. Lew Gantt had not even got his pistol out of the holster.

"It had moss all over it, Martin," Cameron said.

The black eyes glittered in the cold-gray face. "Who are you?" Martin asked. "How do you know me?"

"I'm Smoky Cameron."

"Ah . . ." the fellow said in a long breath. "I can feel a little better about this now." His eyes grew blank. Pain and shock dropped him. His cheek slashed along the hard earth. His hat came off and showed a bald spot at the back of his head. At the wrinkled crook of his right coat sleeve bits of bone from his shattered elbow showed in the bloody fabric.

Lew sensed some of it, just enough to know that he was far out of his class, that years of experience separated him from complete understanding. He knew that he was just a greenhorn who had tried to sit in a high-rolling game. The feeling was heightened when, after Cameron dressed Martin's wound and put him on his horse, Martin went away without another glance at Lew.

Lew heard him tell Cameron, "I sort of got sucked into something, didn't I?"

"You hired out once too often."

It took a good deal of self from Lew's thinking. Sure, they were afraid enough of him to send a killer to drop him and help clear the way to the west hills, but that did not make him feel important. It did not scare him, either. It made him more anxious to go home and ask Stump what he could do to help. Tomorrow his promise to Cameron would be up.

Worry ran the sharp points of restlessness through Lew as he waited for Cameron to return. He offered to start digging the canal for Cranklow.

"Too rainy, Lew," the farmer said. "You just lay low today, and trust your friend."

Cameron came back through the rain that night. He took care of the claybank and ate his supper. He did not have much to say, other than that he had taken Martin to Revelation and turned him over to Sheriff Springer.

"What's the charge?" Cranklow asked.

"No charge. Just holding him. He couldn't go anywhere with that arm, anyway."

Lew felt that a mighty wall of violence was building in the valley, with him not able to understand all the details. When he and Cameron were crossing the rain-greased yard on their way to the haymow, Lew said, "I've decided not to wait the other day. I'm going to start for home tonight."

Cameron did not answer until he was in the mow, struggling out of wet boots. "Tomorrow. We'll win or lose the whole deal tomorrow."

"Is that all you want to say?"

"Yeah."

Lew sat down on his blankets. "Who hired that Martin?"

"I don't know," Cameron said.

It was still raining when they rode out before daylight. Lew figured they would go toward Spur, but they went down-valley instead. Where the roads forked a mile from town, Sheriff Springer was waiting under the cottonwoods. He looked gloomily at water darkening the skirts of his rig, and he showed no enthusiasm for what lay ahead. His slicker rattled as he turned his horse toward Short Fork. There were tracks of five or six horses already in the muddy ruts.

"You were right, Cameron," Springer said. "I got the word that it starts from Short Fork."

"Wigram has got to push Hemphill all the way, but he's pushing a dead horse now. How's Martin?"

"Plug Riddle was taking his arm off when I left. You'd a done him a favor to kill him instead of that."

THE Short Fork yard was full of horses. A poker game was going on in the bunkhouse. The four men lounging out of the rain on the wide front porch of the main building paid little attention to the riders drifting in through the misty drizzle until Lew and his companions were right at the gate. Then someone said, "Oh, oh!" and went quickly into the house.

Custer Wigram was on the porch by the time the three dismounted. The bleak planes of his face were white with anger. Hemphill came out and stood beside him. He was a stocky man with a big shoulder reach and a pug-

186

nacious face that said he was willing to tackle the devil and give him odds; but that only went as deep as his face, which right now was flushed, and more stubborn than determined.

Buck Hodel and Rip Goodwin, followed by nine or ten others, came from the bunkhouse. Hodel was a little pale, Lew observed, but otherwise he seemed all right.

There ought to have been some better way to get things stopped than this, Lew thought. His stomach felt like it was flat against his backbone.

Cameron went out in front of his horse. "You're not taking a gang to Stump Gantt's today, Wigram—or any other day."

Wigram looked at Springer. "How'd *you* get into this?"

"First, because the U. S. Marshal here asked me; second, because he's right." Springer unbuttoned his slicker. He removed it and let it drop in a stiff heap over a puddle of water. Under his corduroy coat he was wearing an old black sweater, with his gun belt buckled over it, and the trim, curving handle of his .45 right in handy reach.

He looked pretty solid and dangerous, Lew thought, and wished he could make some kind of gesture, too; but all Lew could do was gulp at dry cotton in his mouth and try to hold a poker face.

"You're licked, Wigram," Cameron said. "You know it. To start what you want to start you're going to have to kill us three, and you'll have to do it before Hemphill, a man who no longer owns a cow or piece of land in the valley."

Wigram swung his gaunt head toward Hemphill, who stared at the floor of the porch.

"So that's why you backed out!" Wigram said.

Hemphill raised his head. "By God, I've had about enough of your abuse, Wigram! Sure, I sold out! What right I had from use of the land here I relinquished to four farmers. I told you two years ago we couldn't beat this thing."

"You chicken-livered, gutless—"

"Shut up, Wigram, or I'll knock the blisters off that skinny face of yours!" This was a personal affair now.

Even in his rage Wigram realized that. "What'd you do with your cattle?"

"That's none of your business," Hemphill said.

"Buck Hodel, your own foreman, took an option on them, Wigram." Cameron said. "Does that give you an idea of what might have happened to you, if you'd been lucky enough to grab the west hills?"

All Wigram's rage seemed to evaporate, but it was worse than ever inside him, Lew figured, as he watched the Spur owner pace deliberately from the porch and start toward Hodel.

"Is that the truth, Buck?" Wigram asked.

"Just a minute!" Cameron's voice was a hard crack in the tension as men moved away from Hodel, as Spur and Short Fork began to separate. "Lew here has a little business with Hodel first. Hodel is the one who sent for Trey Martin to come in here and kill Gantt."

Hodel was set like a spring. "That's a dirty lie."

"It all came out of Martin—this morning while Plug

Riddle was taking his arm off without chloroform."

Lew saw on Hodel's face that Cameron had bluffed through to the truth. The Spur foreman's mouth loosened. His eyes flicked from side to side. He was alone with hostile men.

"What do you want to do with him, Lew?" Cameron asked in a flat tone.

For a moment Lew did not want to do anything, and then he gathered thoughts about Hodel from here and there, and the feel of watching men helped, and he brought everything into a great cold lump that resembled reason, which said that he must kill Buck Hodel in the name of justice.

He started slowly toward Hodel. This second time would be easy. Hodel was scared tight, so desperate that he would try to do everything at one time—and be wild and helpless. Lew Gantt was cold and sure. For the first time he understood the intangible factors that old Railroad Costigan always claimed were the real weights in a pistol scrap—complete disregard for life; don't think, just shoot.

For three slow steps Lew Gantt was as impersonal as death, a stocky youth with a tight mouth and blue eyes knife-cold with blankness. He was geared to kill, and the rest was nothing but obedience. Then he stopped. The reasons he had summoned fell apart before the trapped look in Hodel's eyes. Habit and training made Lew weigh the forces that pushed him. He remembered the fine green lines of evil in Trey Martin's face. A man could become another Martin too easily.

"I think," he said slowly, "you better get clean out of this country for good, Hodel."

"I'll go," Hodel said.

Cameron made a little nod and something quick ran across his face. He was saying that Lew had done the right thing.

Springer's eyes were pale points under the cliffs of his brows. He did not look at Lew. The tension of a waiting mountain sat in Springer, and Lew wondered why the sheriff did not realize that the backbone of the fight was broken.

Wigram said, "The kid is soft, Buck. But I can't let you go."

"Yes, you will," Springer said suddenly. "It's time I got my spoon into this mess. Hodel is drifting. I'm arresting you, Wigram."

Wigram thought a moment. "What for?" he challenged.

The cone of interest now ran its point between the bulky sheriff and gaunt Wigram, but Lew observed that Springer was only half watching Wigram. And then standing there in the rain beside the tepee of his yellow slicker, Springer drew his gun. The thick fumes of black powder smoke hung in the damp air.

Across the yard Hodel's mouth dropped open. The pistol bearing on Lew fell into a puddle, and then Hodel went down in the mud like a head-shot beef.

Springer looked angrily at Lew. "You can't turn your

back on a man like that. Don't you ever learn nothing?"

"I slipped, too," Cameron said.

Wigram only glanced at Hodel. "You can't arrest me, Springer."

"I know it," the sheriff said. "You're bad beat, though. You got your choice of clearing out or going to Stump Gantt on his own terms if you figure to run cows in the west hills."

"Dead as hell," a Short Fork rider said, turning Hodel over.

"I get paid for it," Springer said bitterly. "Let's get out of here."

The sheriff did not like the mud on his floor, or the way Cameron pushed things aside to sit on a corner of the desk. But he did his best to cover up his feelings. "You put me in for another term, Cameron. Considering the farmer vote that's come in the last two years, I wouldn't have made it this fall."

"Nobody *dragged* you out to Short Fork this morning," Cameron answered.

"Uh-huh." Springer looked at Lew. "I guess I earned my votes all right." In a curiously somber voice he asked Lew: "Do you know what it might have meant if you'd gone over the hump and killed Hodel when you started to?"

"I guessed. It wouldn't have been so good for me."

"Maybe you did learn something down here," Springer said. "Maybe you crossed the line between being a kid and a man. You can go back to Stump now and see how much he's changed."

Cameron's face was dead sober. "You may find that your old man has learned a lot since you been gone."

Springer knew Mark Twain, too, but he had never heard him so aptly quoted. The sheriff forgot the muddy tracks. He made little noise but he was laughing all the way down when Cameron and Lew stepped outside.

"Tell your sis—tell your father—I'll be up in a few days," Cameron said. "Don't forget the rig for that pig-tailed demon. She told me all about it when I was up there. I see just the answer in Bixler's saddle shop every time I go past."

"Yeah. That's where Odalie saw it. I couldn't buy a secondhand saddle blanket now, let alone a silver-trimmed rig."

"Try the bank," Cameron said. "When I start splitting with a man in a poker game I'll know I'm not fit to make an honest living. You must have about two hundred and fifty bucks left." He gave Lew a little shove, and then went back into Springer's office.

For a while Lew stood on the walk with his hat brim drooping lower in the rain. From the corners of his eyes he saw them watching him from inside. It would take a little time to straighten out and sort some of the things which he had learned. But there was no rush.

This rain was going to be mighty good for the grass in the west hills. Lew Gantt went slowly up the street toward Bixler's saddlery.

CAMPAIGNING COWPOKE

By CLARK GRAY

That thumping sound you hear is being made by old-time Western writers turning over in their graves, because, in the only physical-conflict scene in CAMPAIGNING COW-POKE, the hero gets beaten by the villain. Fortunately, however, the hero comes out on top in the end, anyway.

Whether you're a Democrat or a Republican, you'll be amused by the description of Old West politics in this lighthearted, rollicking yarn.

THE two Ferguson boys operated a three-hundred-cow ranch they had inherited from their daddy. The ranch bordered the Canadian River in the Texas Panhandle. The entire place was fenced with six wires and cedar posts. Most of the grass was open; the river gave abundant water and wintertime shelter in the breaks. It was a nice layout, and the Ferguson boys tended to business and made a nice living.

They were lean and friendly young men. Having been brought up with cattle, they knew how to work their calves at the right time to avoid screw-worm infestation. They gentled their old mother cows and kept their fences up and had the horses as tame as pet dogs. Every year they sold about two hundred thirty weanling calves as stockers to the neighbors. Their cull cows, some forty a year, were thrown in with a larger herd and trailed to the Abilene, Kansas, railhead.

The steady one was Dave. Dave was tall and blond, with brown sober eyes. He had married early, a girl as steady and sober as himself. Already they had two saucer-eyed,

193

unsmiling children. Dave stayed at home and tended the mother cows while Red trail-drove to Abilene.

Red wasn't wild in the sense that he drank or gambled or shot up people. He was no hard case. He was freckled and blue-eyed, with a lithe, well-muscled body. But Red believed that along with work, a man was entitled to his fun.

That was why Red wintered over in Abilene and didn't get back to the home stomping-grounds in Roan till the following June. And that, too, was why Ellie Jones threw Red over.

"Ellie," Dave told Red over the supper table on the day of his arrival home, "has got herself engaged to Sheriff Tom Blake. What in blazes kept you so long, Red?"

Red stuffed a forkful of fried round steak into his mouth and grinned. He had a grin that could charm the ears off a sow.

"Ever been in Abilene in wintertime, Dave? The floating population's all gone then. Only the gamblers and the barkeeps left. And the girls." He winked. "I got myself a job in a feed store and spent the winter making friends."

Dave shook his head and sighed. "You've lost Ellie while you've been tomcatting around. You can't expect a girl like that to wait forever, Red. And you won't get her back. Tom Blake will make trouble if you try."

"Tom Blake," Red opined, "is too old for Ellie. And too fat. Ellie wouldn't like a lazy husband, Dave."

Dave shrugged. His sober eyes had a faraway look, the look of a man weighing his responsibilities. Then he smiled and punched Red affectionately on the arm.

"We've always stuck together, Red. I reckon we always will. I think I know how you feel about Ellie. You let me know how you come out."

Red bought a box of lemon drops at Roan Mercantile. He got a barbering job, and about eight o'clock he was walking up the boardwalk toward Lawyer Jones's house with his lean shoulders swaying jauntily and his Stetson hat cocked a little to one side. He didn't anticipate any trouble with Ellie, for he had been courting her off and on since they'd been in the eighth grade together. He knew Ellie like an old shoe. Of late he'd caught himself wondering why he didn't marry her and get it over with.

He found Ellie on the front-porch steps and right away he began making up his lost ground. It was a thing Red was good at. Before long he was sitting pretty close to Ellie, there on the step in the moonlight. That was when Sheriff Blake came stalking through the picket gate and up the plank walk.

"Heard you were back in town," Tom Blake greeted. Blake was a paunchy man ten years older than Red and Ellie. He halted before them and put his hands on his hips and scowled. Moonlight carved out the black outline of a holster at his side. It sparked bluely off the handcuffs hanging from his belt. "Get out of here, Red."

Red Ferguson grinned at Ellie. His voice was a trifle cool. "Maybe he thinks I'm his dog."

"Get moving." Tom Blake said. "Ellie's engaged to me."

Red unwound his lean body and came slowly to his feet, still grinning.

He said, "Now, Tom, I came here on a friendly visit. I reckon it's up to Ellie to tell me when to leave."

"All right." Tom Blake turned gruffly to Ellie. "Tell him to scat, hon!"

Ellie Jones's pretty face turned from one man to the other. She was a small, dark girl dressed in white. She touched her hair with a dainty hand, an instinctively feminine gesture, Red thought. Now, being a lawyer's daughter, Ellie had been very properly brought up. She knew how to cook and sew and keep household accounts, which was the correct field of knowledge for a nice young girl. But it appeared to Red that she was not above a little feminine enjoyment of this kind of thing. She smiled sweetly and impartially.

"You're my guests." Her voice had a silky touch of command, and she patted the porch step on either side. "Sit down, both of you."

Stubbornly Tom Blake shook his head. He was a big man with a one-track mind. "I ain't going to do it. I came here to visit my future wife, not to listen to some jakeleg cowpuncher." He glowered at Red. "I got a notion to teach you some manners, bucko."

Red Ferguson shifted a little on his feet. He was still smiling; his mop of hair was a little mussed in the moonlight. He had known he'd have to make this decision about Tom Blake sooner or later. Cheerfully he made it now.

"It ain't polite to refuse that kind of invite, is it Tom? Leave your gun with Ellie."

He heard Ellie suck in her breath sharply, but he ignored it. Turning, he stalked around the house and out the gate into the alley. He heard Tom Blake's gruff voice as the sheriff ordered Ellie into the house. Presently Blake joined him in the alley. Blake's big shoulders looked blocky as hams in the shifting light of the alley.

"Bucko," he said, "I'm going to cut your face up so you won't want to see Ellie for a while."

"Come ahead," Red said, and when Tom Blake charged Red hit him in his soft stomach, burying his fist to the wrist.

He heard Blake's grunt of dismay; then Blake half spun away and Red saw him grasping for something at his belt. Red thought of the handcuffs, but he didn't believe it. Then he couldn't help but believe it, for he caught the shine of them as Blake got them free and hefted them to strike.

Red ducked, but not far enough. The slashing cuffs caught him on the back of the neck, driving him to his knees and flinging an array of gaudy lights across his vision. He tried to get up, and he sensed that Tom Blake was striking again with the steel cuffs. ...

He awoke on an iron cot, in a barred cell. He came erect, groaning, feeling pain in his face. He prodded gingerly at his nose, and there was a deep cut there. Then a shadow fell across him.

"Come on," a voice said.

Red looked up to see Tom Blake standing outside the bars. Blake was freshly shaved; he was smoking a cigar.

Red said wryly, "You meant it, didn't you—about cutting me up?"

"Come on," Tom Blake said. "I want to see you in my office."

Red got up painfully and followed Blake through the cell door, down the corridor. A half-dozen deputies loafed outside Blake's office. They stared curiously, but at Blake's curt words of dismissal they drifted off. Inside the office Blake sank into a swivel chair and put his spurred boots on top of his desk.

"Set," Blake said.

Red Ferguson sat. He took note of a few things. The deputies, for instance, who had been loafing in the corridor. The bagged canvas seat of Blake's swivel chair. The long scratch marks on Blake's desk where the sheriff had raked his spurs. The foul scent of stale cigars that filled the room.

Red said, "You must spend a lot of time here."

Tom Blake knocked cigar ash on the floor. "Red, I could book you for disturbing the peace. I ain't going to do it—this time. But you'll have to behave from here on out. Understand?"

Red said, "I understand all right, Tom. I never knew you was afraid of competition."

"I ain't." Tom Blake grinned around his cigar. "I know how to handle it."

Red Ferguson touched his chin. There was another cut place there, where the cuffs had struck him after he had lost consciousness.

"You sure do—Tom, ain't there an election this fall?"

Blake's eyes narrowed. "What about it?"

Red Ferguson tried a tentative smile. It hurt his mouth, but he kept on smiling anyway. He said, "I don't think you do enough work, Tom. You set there in that swivel chair and smoke cigars and let your deputies run around on your chores. And you've got twice as many deputies as any sheriff in Roan ever had before. That ain't good. Costs the county too much."

He turned and went out, leaving Tom Blake staring at him. He got his horse and rode home.

Dave was shoeing a pony in the cattle pens when Red rode by on the way to the house. Red didn't stop, but he saw Dave lower the pony's forefoot to wave, saw Dave's mouth drop open at the sight of his cut-up face. At the house Red went to his room and began to sponge the dried blood from his face with a wet towel.

Dave came in. Red saw that his brother's face was dark with anger. Dave had gone to his own room and got a gun. The gun strapped at Dave's lean hip did not look natural there.

"Who did it?" Dave said.

Red looked at Dave over the towel without speaking for a moment. He dabbed cautiously at his eye. Dave asked harshly:

"Was it Blake?"

Red put down the towel. "Dave, it was Blake. But I'll square this in my own way. I'm going to run for sheriff."

Dave sat down heavily on the bed. He shook his head. He glanced up at Red and studied him as if he were a queer species of critter, then shook his head again. For the first time Red noticed with a pang that Dave really looked like an older brother, with the worried eyes, the little lines of age on his cheeks, everything.

Dave said, "That's a damned crazy thing to do!"

Red nodded. "Would you rather I'd take after him with a gun?"

"But suppose you win?" Dave protested. "You might actually get elected."

"I damned well aim to get elected."

Dave got up and walked to the window, hands behind his back. Red poked at his face with the towel and watched Dave's hands clasp and unclasp, and he was sorry that he'd had to upset Dave.

"Red, I'll be glad when you marry Ellie and settle down." Dave said wearily.

"One thing at a time, Dave. When's the closing date for filing?"

"Couple days." Dave sighed. "You won't have much time to campaign. The primary's less than a month off."

"Then I won't meet him in the primary. I'll file on the Republican ticket. That way I have till November to beat him."

"The Republican ticket!" Dave turned and looked at Red, and he began to laugh. "Boy, you been in Abilene too long. This here is Texas. You couldn't get elected flea-scratcher on the Republican ticket."

Red grinned, not minding it when Dave laughed at him. "You watch me."

Dave said, "I'll watch you, all right, Red. But hell, I kind of hate to vote Republican myself, even for you. It just ain't the custom in Texas." Thoughtfully he knuckled his blond head. "Look, you go see Phineas Jones, Ellie's dad. He's a Republican, if I remember right—the only man I ever heard own up to it. Go see what he says."

Red did go to see Phineas Jones. He found him in his office, a starchy, prunelike little man with a stiff white collar. Jones became somewhat wistful when Red stated his business.

"I wish I could advise you to run on our ticket, Red. But the fact is you'd never live it down. People would laugh at you the rest of your life. Not that I wouldn't like to see you run, mind! I'm only thinking of your own good."

Red said, "How do I get on the ticket?"

"Hell, I can take care of that for you. There's not even enough Republicans in the county to fill out the slate. If you want the sheriff's nomination, all you got to do is say so."

"Will you help me campaign?"

"Sure." An eager light replaced the wistfulness in Phineas Jones's face. "I'll figure the issues for you. How do you feel about the tariff, Red? And you're for hard money, I take it?"

"I don't know if I'm for hard money or not," Red said. "I thought all money was hard, except paper money. I don't know about such things, Mr. Jones. All I know is that Tom Blake is a Democrat. That makes me a Republican."

Phineas Jones sighed. "I guess that's as good a reason as most folks have. All right, Red, I'll get you filed. You'll begin to campaign next week."

Red found out about campaigning, and he didn't like the things he found out. He had thought vaguely about

201

making speeches, about getting his picture in the Roan *Weekly Gazette*. But Phineas Jones laughed wryly at those ideas.

"The ways to campaign," Jones said, "is to go talk in person to every qualified voter in the country. Back him in a corner and argue with him. Convince him you're the man for the job."

Red blinked his dismay. "All of 'em! There must be hundreds!"

"Two thousand three hundred and forty-two," Jones said. "I can cross a couple hundred party regulars off the list, because they'd vote Democratic if the devil himself was a candidate." Phineas Jones sighed. "I wish there was some Republicans like that in Texas."

Red grinned. "What'll I tell the others?"

"I'll work it out for you. But remember this, son. It ain't so much what you say as it is the way you say it. You got to turn on the personality. You got to shine." Phineas Jones turned to spit into a big brass cuspidor, and he did not look happy.

Red spent the next few days in Phineas Jones's office, memorizing the gist of what Jones wrote out for him on long legal sheets of paper. The duties of a county sheriff, his own qualifications, the aspects in which Tom Blake had failed to do a good job. Phineas Jones even went out and did a little snooping for him at the courthouse and the bank, and he came back with some facts that made Red grunt in surprise. Red copied down the facts with grim pleasure.

The Sunday night before he was to start campaigning

he went to see Ellie with a handful of roses from the picket fence around the home ranch.

Ellie came to the door with a smile. The smile disappeared and her eyes darkened when she recognized him.

"You came to see Father?"

Red shook his head and extended the roses with a grin. "I came to see you, Ellie. Can I come in?"

She bit her lip and stared a long moment at the half-healed cuts on his face. Suddenly her eyes filled with tears.

"Oh, Red! Why did you have to pull a gun on Tom?"

Red lost his grip on the roses and almost dropped them. "Why did I what?" His voice was harsh.

"Pull that derringer out of your hat? Tom wouldn't have hurt you like that if you'd fought fair."

Red said grittily, "Tom told you I pulled a derringer?"

She nodded in silent misery. "He had to tell me, Red. He didn't want me to think he'd used the cuffs on you without cause."

Red felt a sudden sharp pain in his hand; he realized he was gripping the roses so tightly a thorn had pierced his thumb. He said gently, "And you believe him?"

"Of course." There was a kind of pride in the erectness of her shoulders. "Tom may have his faults, Red. But lying isn't one of them."

"Isn't it?" Red took the roses and separated them in his hands, staring at them without seeing them, sorting his bitter thoughts. At length he sighed.

"Ellie, you're a nice girl, and you think nice things about people. But you don't know the truth about Tom Blake. I hope I can show you the truth before you marry him."

203

Red began to campaign next morning. He strapped his warbag behind his saddle and rode toward the far end of the county, stopping at every farmhouse on his way. To every voter he told his story.

Tom Blake, Red said grimly, had fifteen deputies on the county pay roll. Never in the history of Roan County had any sheriff before Blake hired more than seven. What did those extra eight deputies do? Red asked. He left it to the voter to remember the way those deputies hung around the courthouse.

And where, Red argued, did Tom Blake get the money in his bank account? Red pulled out the figures Phineas Jones had given him and read them off. A bank account of five thousand dollars. A new house in town that cost three thousand if it cost a nickel. A ranch south of Roan. Blake had acquired these things since he had become sheriff. Could it be that Blake was taking kickbacks from his deputies?

These were telling arguments, because they were true. It was also true, Red suspected, that too many drunks had been rolled in Roan saloons lately. But he had no proof of that.

Sometimes Red got a promise of votes. More often the man would say:

"Maybeso, Mister. But my pappy and grandpappy would turn over in their graves if I voted for a Republican."

Red would grin then. "Don't you believe in voting for the best man?"

"Sure," the voter would answer. "But if he was a Republican, how could he *be* the best?"

Red stayed out for a month in that section of the county, seeing some eight hundred voters. He grew gaunt with the constant travel and the irregular hours. His stomach became upset now and then from eating strange food, and he found it a little harder to maintain his cheerful grin. It was late July when he got back into Roan to find that he had been right about the drunks.

"It's been a regular crime wave," Phineas Jones reported. "A man don't dare take more'n three drinks or he wakes up in the alley with his pockets empty. It's hard to prove it on Tom Blake's deputies, but they're always hanging around."

"Do you suppose," Red said, "that those deputies are kicking back part of that to Blake?"

"Hell, yes, I suppose it," Phineas Jones snapped peevishly. "Rolling drunks is a crime, ain't it? How else would them deputies get away with it without Blake's knowledge and permission? And Blake wouldn't give that permission without a good reason. And money is a damned good reason."

Red said, "How's Blake taking the campaign?"

Phineas Jones looked embarrassed. "He's laughing like hell, Red. He thinks it's funny to have a Republican running against him. Matter of fact, I think that's another reason why he's letting his deputies roll so many drunks. It's sort of a taunt, you might say. But he could go too far. If we could only get some proof about those kickbacks—"

"How's Ellie?" Red asked.

Phineas Jones took out a stubby pipe and stuffed it with slender old fingers. "Red, you know the girl as well as I do, maybe better. She got engaged to Blake while you was prowlin' around Abilene. It might have been to show you she was independent—I don't know. Anyway, she's got her pride up now, and neither you nor I can help her there."

Red said, "All right. I'll head south next week."

He spent three days helping Dave cut out and sell some two hundred weanling calves. He found that Dave, too, knew about the drunks.

"Them deputies," Dave said, "ain't Texas boys, Red. You can tell by listening to 'em talk. There's a different accent for every man of 'em."

Red grinned. "It ain't polite to listen to a man's accent, Dave. Some folks are kind of shy about letting on where they come from."

"That's what I was getting at." Dave's usually placid face was lined with worry. "Red, did you ever stop to think about where Tom Blake gets his deputies?"

Red looked up at Dave sharply. He said, "No, Dave, I never did think about it. But I'm thinking about it now." He slapped Dave on the shoulder with the flat of his hand. "You ain't as simple as you look, son."

Red rode south and spent two more months campaigning. He found that the temper of the populace was changing. News of the goings-on in Roan had spread out into the rural areas, where Tom Blake's vote-getting strength was greatest, among the church-going, God-fearing people.

"I can't figure it," one leather-faced old cattleman told Red. "Tom Blake's a religious man. Him and me are deacons in the same church. I can't believe he's a part of this small-time skulduggery. But if he ain't, how come nobody's been arrested?"

Red Ferguson nodded understandingly. "Most politicians put up a front, I reckon. Tom Blake is a deacon because it gets him votes. But pretending to be pure don't change the actual smell of a man, does it?" His young jaw hardened. "You'll see an honest job done, if I'm elected."

He began to feel that he was making progress after that. Not much, but a little. Tom Blake, he decided, wasn't playing his cards close enough to his vest. Blake was overconfident, counting too much on a solid Democratic vote.

The feeling grew as the weeks passed and the first frosts of October put a chill in the clear morning air. Voters talked a little less of party loyalty now. They began to ask more pointed questions about Tom Blake. Some of the questions Red couldn't answer, for he had no absolute proof. If he only had proof—The thought sent him into deep concentration one night as he sat beside his lonely campfire with his back propped against his saddle.

Next day Red reached the little railroad community of Blackbird, in the south end of the county. There he went to the brick railroad station. He wrote two telegrams. The first read:

Sheriff Tom Blake, Roan, Texas.
Your list and description of Roan County deputies received. Incomplete investigation shows rewards outstand-

ing for at least six of your men. Will arrive Roan to make necessary arrests within few days. Your claim to rewards on these men acknowledged.—TIM O'SHANTER, *Texas Ranger.*

Red kept a copy of the telegram and gave another copy to the station agent for immediate dispatch. Then, grinning, he reread his second telegram:

Sheriff Tom Blake, Roan, Texas.
Arriving Roan today on 3:22 northbound.

—O'SHANTER.

Red gave his second telegram to the station agent. "Keep this one till you hear from me, will you, Mister?"

The station agent was a burly man with one ear half shot away. His lips moved as he read the second telegram.

"And keep your mouth shut," Red added. "This here is confidential business."

The agent folded the second telegram and put it carefully in his pocket. His mouth was grim. "I come from Kansas, Ferguson. A Mississippi Democrat shot off this ear during the war. Anything else you need?"

Red's blue eyes crinkled in a sympathetic smile. Then he nodded. "You might ask the agent in Roan to see that one of Blake's deputies gets hold of this first telegram. Accidental-like you know. Can you trust him to do that?"

"I reckon. He's my son."

Red grinned and paid the man. He left Blackbird at a gallop, heading directly home.

He arrived in town shortly after noon next day. As he crossed the tracks and turned his pony's nose toward the business district, he heard a gunshot. The figure of a big man cut through the cottonwoods and across the sandy street three blocks ahead at a dead run. Sunlight flashed from the handcuffs at the figure's belt.

Red Ferguson saw the running man duck into Phineas Jones's office building, and he grinned and swung his pony around toward the railroad station. The action had started a little quicker than he'd figured. Dismounting, he spoke quickly to the youth behind the counter.

"Get in touch with your pa. Have him send on that other telegram to Blake. When it comes through, you deliver it yourself to Phineas Jones's office, pronto. Got it?"

The youngster nodded solemnly. His eyes were big with excitement and curiosity, but Red had no time for explanations now. He ran back to his pony at a lope.

By the time Red had reached Phineas Jones's office building, the deputies had gathered. They stood in the middle of the street under the cottonwoods, all fifteen of them. Fifteen dark-faced men, some tall, some short and fat, some light and some dark, but all alike in the guns they wore and in the grim determination in their eyes. Red halted before them.

"Tom Blake around?"

The tallest of the deputies nodded. "Up in Jones's office."

Red took a look around. The street seemed empty, but it wasn't. There were faces peering out of windows and around doors and behind blinds all up and down Main Street, from the mercantile and the barbershop and the saloon and the blacksmithy and the bank.

Red lit a cigarette and puffed out the match. "Something wrong, boys?"

The tall deputy shook his head. "You go up and find Blake, Ferguson. Tell him we want to see him."

"What about?"

"That," the tall deputy answered coolly, "is private. But you tell Blake it won't be private long, if he don't come out."

Red shrugged. "Okay, boys." He moved to the hitch-rack and dismounted and went up the stairway to Phineas Jones's office.

He found Phineas seated in his swivel chair, with Tom Blake standing over him. Phineas's mouth was opening and closing soundlessly; he was very pale. Tom Blake was talking, his big voice booming through the room, which was why he hadn't heard Red's entry. Blake's gun was on his hip.

"You started it," Blake was roaring. "You and that damned redhead cowpuncher, with that fake telegram. Now end it!"

Red grinned and tiptoed across the room and lifted Blake's gun from holster. He flipped the gun to Phineas Jones as Blake whirled with a startled oath. Phineas caught the gun skillfully and turned it on Blake, and a little color returned to his prunelike face.

Red said, "A little trouble with the boys, Tom?"

Blake licked his lips. He lifted his right hand to the

handcuffs in his belt, then after a thoughtful moment dropped it.

"Damn you to hell, Ferguson! One of my deputies took a shot at me!"

Red grinned. "Lucky I got back to town. I'll fix everything for you, Tom."

Still grinning, he went to the window. Outside he saw that the deputies had scattered a little, behind the shelter of the horse trough and the cotton-woods in the middle of the street. The boy from the railroad station was coming up the boardwalk with a yellow envelope in his hand now.

Red spotted the tall deputy staring at him from the mercantile porch. He cupped his hands around his mouth and shouted:

"Blake claims you boys owe him some money. Says he only wants to collect what's coming to him."

He heard Tom Blake's inarticulate curse, but he ignored that. He watched the bafflement, and the anger, twist the gaunt face of the deputy.

"That dirty lying son!" the deputy shouted hoarsely. "That cooks him with me, Ferguson. I won't cover up for him no more. I paid him ten percent of my salary, and so did the rest of the boys. When that wasn't enough, we went out in the alleys and got more. Send the penny-pinchin' coyote down, or by Ned, we're comin' after him!"

The sigh that came up from the town then was plainly audible. Behind the doors and windows and curtains voices spoke excitedly to one another. Out of the corner of his eye Red saw Ty Corbett, the newspaper editor, break from the bank and run at a crouch across the street toward the office of the Roan *Weekly Gazette*.

At that moment there came a knock on Phineas Jones's door, and Red turned to see Tom Blake sputtering helplessly under the gun in Jones's gnarled hand. Jones himself was scratching his head in pop-eyed bewilderment.

"Red, I don't savvy how you done it! Or how you're going to keep Blake from getting killed!"

"You will, Phineas." Red went to the door and took the telegram the youth handed him. He read it aloud.

"Arriving Roan today on 3:22 northbound.

—O'SHANTER."

Grinning, Red crumpled the telegram and tossed it out the window. He watched the wind catch the yellow paper as it fell past the cottonwoods to strike on the far side of the street. There was a little scuffle in the sand over there; one of the deputies made a dive for the telegram and got it and ran quickly back behind the horse trough.

Red turned to Phineas. "How's Ellie?"

Phineas Jones's eyes were brooding. He shook his head with a sigh. "All right. She broke it off with Blake, here, a couple days ago. Confound it, Red, I don't know what in blazes you've done, but—"

"I've done nothing," Red said, "but send a couple innocent telegrams from a man that doesn't exist." He grinned. "You know, Phineas, it's a funny thing about snakes. Snakes don't trust each other. Every snake among 'em thinks that the other snakes are going to act like snakes." He eyed Tom Blake gravely. "Ain't it so, Tom?"

He moved to the window before Tom Blake could answer. Down in the street he saw the group of deputies clustered around the tall one, who had the wrinkled telegram in his hand. They were conferring excitedly, arguing. A moment later they separated, and as Red Ferguson faced back toward the room, he heard the rapid beat of galloping hoofs heading out of town.

Red wasn't smiling now as he advanced toward Tom Blake. Being an easy-going, soft-hearted young man, he felt a little sorry for Blake. But he didn't let that sorrow change his mind.

"Tom," he said, "I reckon you know this finishes you here. Everybody in Roan heard that deputy admit kicking back part of his salary to you. I'm going to boot you out of town, Tom."

Tom Blake's cheeks seemed to cave in. But the man still had bluster. "You can't run me out of town, Ferguson. Just because a lying deputy spouts some crazy tale—"

"We could call a grand jury," Red interrupted calmly. "We could let them decide whether the deputy was lying. Take your choice, Tom. A penitentiary sentence — or leave town."

Tom Blake's heavy face was mottled with red splotches. But his eyes darkened with defeat, and he dropped his glance, and his voice, when he spoke, was sullen.

"My property?"

"I'll sell it at a sheriff's sale," Red said. "And send you the money."

Nobody was on the street when Red and Tom Blake

came out of Phineas Jones's office and crossed toward the courthouse, where Blake's horse stood at the hitch rail. But Red knew that the eyes behind the doors and windows and curtains were still there. He could feel them, and he had no doubt from the rigid whiteness of Tom Blake's face that Blake felt them, too. Blake walked with his eyes straight ahead and unseeing, like a man walking toward the gallows.

Red waited gravely until Tom Blake got into his saddle. Then he said:

"I think you'd be happier outside of Texas, Tom."

Tom Blake nodded bitterly. His lips made a thin, bloodless line. He turned his horse and rode out of town.

The election went off very smoothly. It was true that Blake's name was still on the ballot, but Blake was no longer a resident of Roan County, and everybody knew it. Of eighteen hundred thirty-two votes cast, Red Ferguson received eighteen hundred thirty-two.

Phineas Jones became wildly enthusiastic. "We had to disgrace a Democrat to do it," he said, waving his pipe, "but we finally elected a Republican in Texas! This is the beginning, boy! With you in office we can build an organization now. Someday we'll put Texas in the marching columns of the Grand Old Party, and you and I will be responsible. Don't that make you feel proud, boy? Think of being the father of all those good Republicans!"

Red Ferguson grinned. "I don't want to be the father of a whole stateful of Republicans, Mr. Jones. Ellie says she only wants to have three."

THE SOUND OF GUNFIRE

By JOHN O'REILLY

THE SOUND OF GUNFIRE is the story of a man who is probably the most unusual hero in Western fiction history: a gunman who is totally blind. Curiously enough, his blindness isn't as much of a handicap as you'd think. In a gunfight after dark, a blind man is on more familiar territory than his enemies. . . .

HE rode into town on a sunless day with the sky as grey as the streaks in his hair, and he swung out of the saddle where a group of rannies were talking in front of the saloon. He wasn't much over thirty-five, despite the grey hair, and he had a tanned, bony face, slightly haggard, and strange-looking eyes. They were grey, too, and completely blank and expressionless, and they didn't waver or move when he sidestepped the other men and walked through the batwings.

"I'm looking for McCord," he told the barkeep. "This his place?"

There was a big sign outside the saloon which said *McCord's*, and a couple of *No Credit* notices signed with McCord's name behind the bar. The keep stared at the grey-haired man for a moment, then guffawed and slammed a dirty hand on the bar.

"No education, huh?" He jerked a thumb at the signs. "Can't you read, pard?"

The man reached forward, took hold of the bartender's

shirtfront, and pulled him across the bar. His expression-less eyes stared straight ahead. "You can't read when you're blind, mister. Get McCord."

He released the keep and listened to his footsteps move down the length of the saloon. A minute later he heard two pairs of feet returning, and one of them moved into position next to him.

"Nice to meet you, McCord," he said softly.

The man next to him had a deep, harsh voice, "How do you know I'm McCord?"

"Easy," the grey-eyed man said. "You fit your description. Tall, maybe six-four, heavy, smooth-shaven."

"The keep told me you were blind."

"I've been blind for years," the stranger said. "Enough years so it doesn't matter. . . .

"When I talked to the barkeep, I smelled his stinking rotgut breath right in my nose, which makes him slightly taller than I am—say six-three. His head didn't touch the drape when he walked into your room in the back but I heard the drape rustle up high when you walked out—so you're taller. Heavy, too—easy to tell that by the way your feet hit the floor. And smooth-shaven—you rubbed your jaw a minute ago, and I heard a rasping sound instead of the soft one you get when you stroke hair."

"You're guessing," the other man said.

"I don't guess about things like that." the blind man said. "A school-teacher I used to know told me it's called the law of compensation—Nature providin' that when a man loses one sense another gets twice as strong. That's the way it is with me—I can hear things no one else can hear. That's why I know you're rolling a smoke on heavy brown paper. White paper has a softer sound."

McCord shook his head. "Very interesting, mister," he said. "Very interesting. You learn something every day." He paused. "But what I want to know is, what's it got to do with me?"

"I'm just statin' my qualifications, McCord. Fact is, I rode into town to do a job for you."

"What kind of job?"

The blind man leaned forward. "I hear tell," he said, "that you want Johnny Hale dead."

McCord's hand jerked, and his whisky glass tumbled to the floor. It shattered loudly, and there was silence for a minute. Then McCord said: "You're crazy."

"Sane as any gunfighter," the blind man said. "My price, McCord, is one thousand dollars."

"I tell you you're crazy," McCord said hoarsely. "And even if I did want somebody killed, what kind of hired gun would *you* make? A blind man—you wouldn't even know where to shoot."

The grey-eyed man laughed, a laugh as unhumorous and unemotional as his eyes. "McCord," he said, "I've been listening to your clock on the wall there ever since I came into this place. You've probably never noticed it, but the pendulum makes one sound when it swings to the right, and another when it swings to the left." His gun flashed in his hand, and a bullet tore the pendulum neatly off its mount. "It was swinging to the right that time."

He laughed again. "How about it, McCord?"

There was another dead silence. Then McCord said,

217

chokingly, "Out. Get out, and don't come into this place again."

Smiling gently, the blind man walked out of the saloon.

Johnny Hale's office was an airless little room just beyond the schoolhouse, a desk and two chairs in back of a rusty-hinged door with *Sheriff* scrawled on it in crude black letters. The blind man went there directly, his nostrils twitching slightly as he approached the desk. "Hale around?"

"Me," the man behind the desk said. He didn't sound like much more than a button, maybe a few years over voting age. It was the way the blind man had figured he would sound, from his description: unruly sandy hair, kid's face with a couple of freckles on the bridge of his nose, wide grin. "What can I do for you?"

"Nothing much," the blind man said. His long fingers found the empty chair and he sat down. "I just thought we ought to meet, seein' I've been volunteerin' to kill you."

Hale's breath whooshed out in a rush. "Say that again."

The blind man smiled. "I've just been down to McCord's saloon, tellin' McCord my price to put a bullet in you is a thousand dollars. Cheap, too, considerin' the prices some hired guns draw."

Hale jumped to his feet and came around the desk. He thrust his face close to the blind man's. "What is this, mister—some kind of joke?"

"No joke a-tall," the grey-eyed man said casually. "Word's pretty general all around this territory that Mc-

Cord is out to get you, and I just sorta thought I'd get *my* bid in. Honest shootin' work is scarce these days, Johnny." He paused. "Want to make a counter-offer on McCord's gizzard, son?"

He could feel Hale staring hard at him. "I'll counter-offer you right into the hoosegow in a minute," the Sheriff said slowly. "I don't need any hired gunnies to do my work for me. I'll get McCord before he gets me—but I'll do it legal."

"Got grounds, Johnny?"

"None of your business," Hale snapped. He paused. "Well, maybe it is, if you're with McCord." His hands slapped the leather of his holsters. "Mister, I'm so close to pinnin' cattle-stealin' on McCord that you'd better make your play right now, if you're going to make it at all. Couple more days, and you'll have to take your pay out of McCord's pocket while he's hangin' from the end of a rope."

The blind man grinned. "Easy, son, easy—don't get your temper up. Right now everything's still in what you might call the negotiation stage." He got to his feet, his hands away from his sides. "I'm sure glad you're close to the proof, Johnny. Your ideas on the subject are no secret around town, you know, and it would be kind of embarrasin' if you were accusin' the wrong guy."

Hale swore. "McCord's behind all the cattle-rustlin' in the last couple of months, all right; I'm not the kind of hombre who talks without reason."

The blind man smiled again, and walked to the door. "That's what I kinda figgered," he said. Then he turned.

"Guess you've noticed by now that I'm a sorta nosy bird," he said. "One more question, son: you happen to have your own ranch?"

Hale stared at him. "Huh? Me? No, course not—sheriffin's my full-time job. It's all I can do hangin' around town keepin' things orderly."

"That's what I figgered, too,'" the blind man said. His blank eyes stared at the Sheriff for a moment. "Well, so long, son—maybe I'll be seeing you again soon."

He thought it would come the moment he passed the schoolhouse, which was still lighted, but the pressure against his eyes lessened and he knew the light had gone out just as he reached it. Then he stopped. The light footsteps he had heard leaving the schoolhouse were running toward him, and when he heard a girl's voice say, "Bill! Bill Reynolds!"—the same voice, grown-up now, but with the familiar quality of sweetness—he knew it was Lorna Stone.

He turned and said, "Been a long time, hasn't it?"

She was in his arms and her lips touched his before she answered. "Almost eight years," she said. "Eight years —but you came right away."

"Us blind fellers ain't kept too busy, Lorna," he said softly. "Anyway, I wanted to know if you grew up the way I figgered...."

He heard the swift intake of her breath. "Your—your eyes, Bill. How can you....?"

"Lots of ways, Lorna," he said. "That perfume, for instance—not the strong, smelly stuff some gals wear—but

220

soft and gentle and just right. And the fact that you're at the schoolhouse—takes courage to take a job as unpopular as book-learnin' out here." He reached out and touched her hair. "And your hair's long and soft, and probably just as red as when—I used to be able to see it. You're a beautiful girl, Lorna."

Her voice was strained when she answered. "Johnny— Johnny Hale, the boy I'm going to marry—he says I am."

The blind man's face lost its smile. "I've just been talkin' to him, Lorna—and I'm afraid your letter was right. That boy *is* usin' his mouth too much. . . ."

"Then you think—"

"That McCord *isn't* behind the rustling?" he finished for her. "No, Lorna, I think Hale's right about that. But he's still talkin' too much." He paused. "Lorna, there's something I've got to tell you. . . ."

There was a sudden sharp crackling sound in the brush down the road. He said rapidly, "I'll have to save it. Lorna, honey, get into that schoolhouse and stay there until I come for you. Quick!"

She started to protest. "Bill," she said. . . .

"Inside. You wrote that I was the only friend you could turn to. Inside, before you don't have any at all."

When she entered the schoolhouse, he started to walk forward. Might as well get under way, and over.

The shot came just when he knew it would—the moment he stepped away from the darkened schoolhouse into the area which pressure on his eyes told him was lighted. For a moment, he felt wild, muscle-stiffening fear, the way he had felt as a kid when owlhoots killed his mother and dad and fired the bullet which left him alive but blind, and then it passed away. He fell onto his stomach, and his gun leaped forward in his hand.

He fired twice rapidly in the direction of the sound, and heard footsteps running. Then another shot snapped back at him, close, and he knew the other had found cover and was trying to finish his work. He grinned crookedly and leaped back into the darkness.

We're on even ground now, he thought—*maybe not so even, at that. Any fool ought to know better than to tangle with a blind man in the dark, but he won't.*

He waited until another shot came, hitting not so close. Then calmly, methodically, the way a man does a thing he has done often before, he fired again—and heard the familiar coughing, gasping shout. It was the sound of a dying man, choking off into silence.

Casually, the blind man reached out and felt along the ground until he found a fist-sized rock. He flipped it into the air and listened to it land in the soft earth a few feet away.

A bullet whanged metallically against the rock.

So it wasn't over. He fired carefully at the sound, and heard another body drop.

There was a long silence, and he realized that the men across the road were beginning to understand that a gun battle in pitch darkness with a blind man was suicidal. They were firing by guess-work; he was right at home. The blind man heard soft, rapid whispers—three voices—

and they began to run toward him. They came from different directions.

He caught one of them with a bullet in the stomach, and then the other two were upon him. He brought his knife into play.

It was the color of silver and had a long razor-sharp blade, and it came from the blind man's sleeve and moved upward with a tearing movement into the body of the nearest man. The man started to curse and then bubbles of blood cut off his voice, and he made a sound deep in his stomach and rolled over on one side.

The other man twisted out of the way of the knife, and his back fell against the blind man's right hand. The blind man stiffened the hand and pulled it upwards. He rabbit-punched twice, and the man slumped to the ground without a sound.

Calmly, the blind man got to his feet and shot him three times through the chest.

He took a deep breath. "I never do fight fair with killers," he said, and bent down beside the man he'd shot. The man was still alive; thick gasps gurgled through his lips.

"McCord?" the blind man asked.

The dying man didn't answer for a minute. Then his voice, McCord's voice, said, spitting the words out: "Go to hell."

"Not me," the grey-eyed man said. "That's where you're going, McCord, any minute now." he paused. "Why'd you jump me tonight?"

The thick gasps continued; no answer.

"McCord," the blind man said again. "You're checking

out soon. Why don't you tell me?" And then he stopped: McCord wouldn't be answering anyone again.

The blind man sighed and reloaded his gun and cleaned his knife and put them away. Nobody had come at the sound of gunfire. This was on the edge of town, and it wasn't surprising about anybody else—but Johnny Hale should have shown better sense.

Some hombres aren't as smart as a weak-minded cayuse, the blind man thought sadly, and he opened the school-house door and called Lorna. "I was going to tell you about this," he said, "but maybe I'd better show you."

Johnny Hale was at the little cook-stove in the room adjoining his office when Lorna and the grey-eyed blind man entered, and he whirled and let the pan clatter to the floor.

"Don't you ever investigate shooting, Johnny?" the blind man asked.

"Shooting?" the Sheriff said, "I—didn't hear any shooting."

"Son," the blind man said, "your ears would have to be as useless as my eyes to keep you from hearing the shooting that just went on."

"Your eyes?" Hale said. "What's wrong with. . . ."

"Now let's not act damn silly, son," the grey-eyed man said, gently. "It doesn't take much to spot a blind man. I was kind of curious when you didn't say anything when I felt around for a chair, but that, I know now, was because one of McCord's boys beat me to your place and told you about me." He sighed. "You know, it sure would have been more convincing for you to have come running out just before—but I guess you were too sure things would go right to bother."

He heard Hale slump heavily in a chair. "I won't even try to figger out what you're talkin' about."

"Ain't hard to figger, Johnny." the blind man said. "Puttin' it in black and white, there's just two things I don't like: outlaws, and people who try to kill me or get me killed." He rolled a smoke with his left hand and kept his right close to his holster. "It just looks to me like you fit in both those classes."

Hale's answer came in a harsh, bitter voice. "I kind of figured you were a mite loco when you first came in here. Now I'm beginning to think it's a lot more than a mite."

The blind man shook his head sadly. "Aw, now, Johnny," he said, "you shouldn't go calling people names when you know it isn't so. Listen, son, and tell me if I'm shootin' close to the target.

"I first began to figure somethin' was funny when Lorna wrote and told me she was scared of trouble because you'd been tellin' everybody around town that McCord was behind the rustlin', and McCord was tellin' everybody around town he was going to get you. Hell, Johnny, that wasn't as smart a scheme as you thought. . . ."

"You're still talkin' loco," Hale said.

"It'll make sense soon. Your scheme wasn't so smart because, in a wide-open town like this one, a feller like McCord doesn't go around threatenin' things for months without doin' something about it—and a Sheriff doesn't accuse a man of rustlin' unless he's got plenty of proof.

" 'Course, you and I know why you started that talk. You figgered if everybody thought you and McCord was enemies, nobody'd ever connect you together on the cattle-stealin'. Later on, I guess, when there wasn't too much left to rustle, you planned to say you found you were wrong, and apologize." He spat. "Sure must've been awkward when a professional gun like I said I was come up to McCord and offered to do a job on you. . . ."

"Lorna," Hale cut in, his voice suddenly thin and high. "You brought this crazy-man here. Tell him he's wrong; tell him he'll get in trouble spreading stuff like this. . . ."

The blind man felt Lorna's fingers pressing more tightly on his arm. "No, Johnny," she said, slowly, "I'm afraid I can't. I think he's right. I think now that I've known it from the start. . . ."

"All right," Hale said. His words were coming faster now, feverishly, hysteria in them. "If you want to stick with your blind boy-friend there, go ahead—but I tell you he's crazy. Everything he's said is guesswork. . . ."

And then the blind man stepped closer. "It's not guesswork, Johnny," he said. "If you want to fool a man who can't see and has to rely on other senses, you better take baths more often. You told me before that you stay round town and haven't a ranch of your own—but the stink of cattle is all over you.

"Where did you get it if you haven't been rustling with McCord?". . .

Young Hale was fast, the blind man knew that the

moment he heard the slap of hand against leather. He pulled his own gun and, fanning his shots, jerked the trigger three times. He heard his bullets thud into flesh before Hale's first came, awry and heading for the side wall, and he knew Hale would be dead before he hit the floor.

He turned to the red-headed girl. Her body was warm and trembling against him.

"I'm sorry, Lorna," he said. "It would have happened to him sooner or later, anyway."

He put his arm gently around her waist. "I'll take you home," he said, "You'll feel better later on. . . ."

"No," she said. "Not home. There's nothing for me here. I'm going back with you."

They walked out into the clear night air, further and further away from the echoes of the sound of gunfire—and he wanted to tell her that he could not let her come, that he could not let her saddle herself with a blind man. But then she kissed him and he forgot all about it, and somehow the subject never came up after that.

SERGEANT HOUCK

By JACK SCHAEFER

This story, which concludes the collection, poses about as difficult and adult a problem as you'll meet anywhere. What happens when a young woman is captured by Indians, made to mate with one of them, bears his child, and is then rescued by a cavalry troop? Will she be accepted back without blemish by her own people—by her husband? The editor of this anthology considers this story, which gives one possible answer, one of the best he has ever read.

SERGEANT HOUCK stopped his horse just below the top of the ridge ahead. The upper part of his body was silhouetted against the sky line as he rose in his stirrups to peer over the crest. He urged the horse on up and the two of them, the man and the horse, were sharp and distinct against the copper sky. After a moment he turned and rode down to the small troop waiting. He reined beside Lieutenant Imler.

"It's there, sir. Alongside a creek in the next hollow. Maybe a third of a mile."

Lieutenant Imler looked at him coldly. "You took your time, Sergeant. Smack on the top, too."

"Couldn't see plain, sir. Sun was in my eyes."

"Wanted them to spot you, eh, Sergeant?"

"No, sir. Sun was bothering me. I don't think—"

"Forget it, Sergeant. I don't like this either."

Lieutenant Imler was in no hurry. He led the troop

slowly up the hill. The real fuss was fifty-some miles away. Captain McKay was hogging the honors there. Here he was, tied to this sideline detail. Twenty men. Ten would have been enough. Ten and an old hand like Sergeant Houck.

With his drawn saber pointing forward, Lieutenant Imler led the charge up and over the crest and down the long slope to the Indian village. There were some scattered shots from bushes by the creek, ragged pops indicating poor powder and poorer weapons, probably fired by the last of the old men left behind when the young braves departed in war paint ten days before. The village was silent and deserted.

Lieutenant Imler surveyed the ground they'd taken. "Spectacular achievement," he muttered to himself. He beckoned Sergeant Houck to him.

"Your redskin friend was right, Sergeant. This is it."

"Knew he could be trusted, sir."

"Our orders are to destroy the village. Send a squad out to round up any stock. There might be some horses around. We're to take them in." Lieutenant Imler waved an arm at the thirty-odd skin-and-pole huts. "Set the others to pulling those down. Burn what you can and smash everything else."

"Right, sir."

Lieutenant Imler rode into the slight shade of the cottonwoods along the creek. He wiped the dust from his face and set his campaign hat at a fresh angle to ease the crease the band had made on his forehead. Here he was, hot and tired and way out at the end of nowhere with another long ride ahead, while Captain McKay was having it out at last with Grey Otter and his renegade warriors somewhere between the Turkey Foot and the Washakie. He relaxed to wait in the saddle, beginning to frame his report in his mind.

"Pardon, sir."

Lieutenant Imler looked around. Sergeant Houck was standing nearby with something in his arms, something that squirmed and seemed to have dozens of legs and arms.

"What the devil is that, Sergeant?"

"A baby, sir. Or rather, a boy. Two years old, sir."

"How the devil do you know? By his teeth?"

"His mother told me, sir."

"His mother?"

"Certainly, sir. She's right here."

Lieutenant Imler saw her then, standing beside a neighboring tree, shrinking into the shadow and staring at Sergeant Houck and the squirming child. He leaned to look closer. She wore a shapeless, sacklike covering with slits for her arms and head. She was sun-and-windburned dark yet not as dark as he expected. And there was no mistaking the color of her hair. It was light brown and long and coiled in a bun on her neck.

"Sergeant! It's a white woman!"

"Right, sir. Her name's Cora Sutliff. The wagon train she was with was wiped out by a raiding party. She and another woman were taken along. The other woman died. She didn't. The village bought her. She's been in Grey Otter's lodge." Sergeant Houck smacked the squirming boy briskly and tucked him under one arm. He looked straight at Lieutenant Imler. "That was three years ago, sir."

"Three years? Then that boy—"

"That's right, sir."

Captain McKay looked up from his desk to see Sergeant Houck stiff at attention before him. It always gave him a feeling of satisfaction to see this great, granite man. The replacements they were sending these days, raw and unseasoned, were enough to shake his faith in the service. But as long as there remained a sprinkling of these casehardened old-time regulars, the Army would still be the Army.

"At ease, Sergeant."

"Thank you, sir."

Captain McKay drummed his fingers on the desk. This was a ridiculous situation and the solid, impassive bulk of Sergeant Houck made it seem even more so.

"That woman, Sergeant. She's married. The husband's alive—wasn't with the train when it was attacked. He's been located. Has a place about twenty miles out of Laramie. The name's right and everything checks. You're to take her there and turn her over with the troop's compliments."

"Me, sir?"

"She asked for you. The big man who found her. Lieutenant Imler says that's you."

Sergeant Houck considered this expressionlessly. "And about the boy, sir?"

"He goes with her." Captain McKay drummed on the

desk again. "Speaking frankly, Sergeant, I think she's making a mistake. I suggested she let us see that the boy got back to the tribe. Grey Otter's dead and after that affair two weeks ago there's not many of the men left. But they'll be on the reservation now and he'd be taken care of. She wouldn't hear of it; said if he had to go she would, too." Captain McKay felt his former indignation rising again. "I say she's playing the fool. You agree with me, of course."

"No, sir. I don't."

"And why the devil not?"

"He's her son, sir."

"But he's—Well, that's neither here nor there, Sergeant. It's not our affair. We deliver her and there's an end to it. You'll draw expense money and start within the hour."

"Right, sir." Sergeant Houck straightened up and started for the door.

"Houck."

"Yes, sir."

"Take good care of her—and that damn' kid."

"Right, sir."

Captain McKay stood by the window and watched the small cavalcade go past toward the post gateway. Lucky that his wife had come with him to this godforsaken station lost in the prairie wasteland. Without her they would have been in a fix with the woman. As it was, the woman looked like a woman now. And why shouldn't she, wearing his wife's third-best crinoline dress? It was a bit large, but it gave her a proper feminine appearance. His wife had enjoyed fitting her, from the skin out, everything except shoes. Those were too small. The woman seemed to prefer her worn moccasins anyway. And she was uncomfortable in the clothes. But she was decently grateful for them, insisting she would have them returned or would pay for them somehow. She was riding past the window, sidesaddle on his wife's horse, still with that strange shrinking air about her, not so much frightened as remote, as if she could not quite connect with what was happening to her, what was going on around her.

Behind her was Private Lakin, neat and spruce in his uniform, with the boy in front of him on the horse. The boy's legs stuck out on each side of the small, improvised pillow tied to the forward arch of the saddle to give him a better seat. He looked like a weird, dark-haired doll bobbing with the movements of the horse.

And there beside the woman, shadowing her in the midmorning, was that extra incongruous touch, the great hulk of Sergeant Houck, straight in his saddle, taking this as he took everything, with no excitement and no show of any emotion, a job to be done.

They went past and Captain McKay watched them ride out through the gateway. It was not quite so incongruous after all. As he had discovered on many a tight occasion, there was something comforting in the presence of that big man. Nothing ever shook him. You might never know exactly what went on inside his close-cropped skull, but you could be certain that what needed to be done he would do.

They were scarcely out of sight of the post when the boy began squirming. Private Lakin clamped him to the pillow with a capable right hand. The squirming persisted. The boy seemed determined to escape from what he regarded as an alien captor. Silent, intent, he writhed on the pillow. Private Lakin's hand and arm grew weary. He tickled his horse forward with his heels until he was close behind the others.

"Beg pardon, sir."

Sergeant Houck shifted in his saddle and looked around. "Yes?"

"He's trying to get away, sir. It'd be easier if I tied him down. Could I use my belt, sir?"

Sergeant Houck held in his horse to drop back alongside Private Lakin. "Kids don't need tying," he said. He reached out and plucked the boy from in front of Private Lakin and laid him, face down, across the withers of his own horse and smacked him sharply. Then he set him back on the pillow. The boy sat still, very still. Sergeant Houck pushed his left hand into his left side pocket and pulled out a fistful of small hard biscuits. He passed these to Private Lakin. "Stick one of these in his mouth when he gets restless."

Sergeant Houck urged his horse forward until he was beside the woman once more. She had turned her head to watch and she stared sidewise at him for a long moment, then looked straight forward again.

They came to the settlement in the same order: the woman and Sergeant Houck side by side in the lead, Private Lakin and the boy tagging behind at a respectful distance. Sergeant Houck dismounted and helped the woman down and handed the boy to her. He saw Private Lakin looking wistfully at the painted front of the settlement's one saloon and tapped him on one knee. "Scat," he said and watched Private Lakin turn his horse and ride off, leading the other two horses.

Then he led the woman into the squat frame building that served as general store and post office and stage stop. He settled the woman and her child on a preserved-goods box and went to the counter to arrange for their fares. When he came back to sit on another box near her, the entire permanent male population of the settlement was assembled just inside the door, all eleven of them staring at the woman.

". . . that's the one. . . ."

". . . an Indian had her . . ."

". . . shows in the kid. . . ."

Sergeant Houck looked at the woman. She was staring at the floor and the blood was leaving her face. He started to rise and felt her hand on his arm. She had leaned over quickly and clutched his sleeve.

"Please," she said. "Don't make trouble account of me."

"Trouble?" said Sergeant Houck. "No trouble." He stood up and confronted the fidgeting men by the door. "I've seen kids around this place. Some of them small. This one needs decent clothes and the store here doesn't stock them."

The men stared at him, startled, and then at the wide-eyed boy in his clean but patched skimpy cloth covering. Five or six of them went out through the door and disappeared in various directions. The others scattered through the store. Sergeant Houck stood sentinel, relaxed and quiet, by his box, and those who had gone out straggled back, several embarrassed and empty-handed, the rest proud with their offerings. Sergeant took the boy from the woman's lap and stood him on his box. He measured the offerings against the small body and chose a small red checked shirt and a small pair of overalls. He set the one pair of small scuffed shoes aside. "Kids don't need shoes," he said. "Only in winter."

When the coach rolled in, it was empty and they had it to themselves for the first hours. Dust drifted steadily through the windows and the silence inside was a persistent thing. The woman did not want to talk. She had lost all liking for it and would speak only when necessary. And Sergeant Houck used words with a natural economy, for the sole simple purpose of conveying or obtaining information that he regarded as pertinent to the business immediately in hand. Only once did he speak during these hours and then only to set a fact straight in his mind. He kept his eyes fixed on the scenery outside as he spoke.

"Did he treat you all right?"

The woman made no pretense of misunderstanding him. "Yes," she said.

The coach rolled on and the dust drifted. "He beat me once," she said and four full minutes passed before she finished the thought. "Maybe it was right. I wouldn't work."

They stopped for a quick meal at a lonely ranch house and ate in silence while the man there helped the driver change horses. It was two mail stops later, at the next change, that another passenger climbed in and plopped his battered suitcase and himself on the front seat opposite them. He was of medium height and plump. He wore city clothes and had quick eyes and features that seemed small in the plumpness of his face. He took out a handkerchief and wiped his face and took off his hat to wipe all the way up his forehead. He laid the hat on top of the suitcase and moved restlessly on the seat, trying to find a comfortable position.

"You three together?"

"Yes," said Sergeant Houck.

"Your wife then?"

"No," said Sergeant Houck. He looked out the window on his side and studied the far horizon.

The coach rolled on and the man's quick eyes examined the three of them and came to rest on the woman's feet.

"Begging your pardon, lady, but why do you wear those things? Moccasins, aren't they? They more comfortable?"

She shrank back further in the seat and the blood began to leave her face.

"No offense, lady," said the man. "I just wondered—" He stopped. Sergeant Houck was looking at him.

"Dust's bad," said Sergeant Houck. "And the flies this time of year. Best to keep your mouth closed." He looked out the window again, and the only sounds were the

237

running beat of the hoofs and the creakings of the old coach.

A front wheel struck a stone and the coach jolted up at an angle and lurched sideways and the boy gave a small whimper. The woman pulled him onto her lap.

"Say," said the man. "Where'd you ever pick up that kid? Looks like—" He stopped. Sergeant Houck was reaching up and rapping against the top of the coach. The driver's voice could be heard shouting at the horses and the coach stopped. One of the doors opened and the driver peered in. Instinctively he picked Sergeant Houck.

"What's the trouble, soldier?"

"No trouble," said Sergeant Houck. "Our friend here wants to ride up with you." He looked at the plump man. "Less dust up there. It's healthy and gives a good view."

"Now, wait a minute," said the man. "Where'd you get the idea—"

"Healthy," said Sergeant Houck.

The driver looked at the bleak, impassive hardness of Sergeant Houck and at the twitching softness of the plump man. "Reckon it would be," he said. "Come along. I'll boost you up."

The coach rolled along the false-fronted one street of a mushroom town and stopped before a frame building tagged Hotel. One of the coach doors opened and the plump man retrieved his hat and suitcase and scuttled into the building. The driver appeared at the coach door. "Last meal here before the night run," he said.

When they came out, the shadows were long and fresh horses had been harnessed. As they settled themselves again, a new driver, whip in hand, climbed up to the high seat and gathered the reins into his left hand. The whip cracked and the coach lurched forward and a young man ran out of the low building across the street carrying a saddle. He ran alongside and heaved the saddle up on the roof inside the guardrail. He pulled at the door and managed to scramble in as the coach picked up speed. He dropped onto the front seat, puffing deeply. "Evening, ma'am," he said between puffs. "And you, general." He leaned forward to slap the boy gently along the jaw. "And you too, bub."

Sergeant Houck looked at the lean young man, at the faded Levis tucked into high-heeled boots, the plaid shirt, the amiable competent young face. He grunted a greeting, unintelligible but a pleasant sound.

"A man's legs ain't made for running," said the young man. "Just to fork a horse. That last drink was near too long."

"The Army'd put some starch in those legs," said Sergeant Houck.

"Maybe. Maybe that's why I ain't in the Army." The young man sat quietly, relaxed to the jolting of the coach. "Is there some other topic of genteel conversation you folks'd want to worry some?"

"No," said Sergeant Houck.

"Then maybe you'll pardon me," said the young man. "I hoofed it a lot of miles today." He worked hard at his boots and at last got them off and tucked them out of the way on the floor. He hitched himself up and over on the seat until he was resting on one hip. He put an

239

arm on the window sill and cradled his head on it. His head dropped down and he was asleep.

Sergeant Houck felt a small bump on his left side. The boy had toppled against him. Sergeant Houck set the small body across his lap with the head nestled into the crook of his right arm. He leaned his head down and heard the soft little last sigh as drowsiness overcame the boy. He looked sidewise at the woman and dimly made out the outline of her head falling forward and jerking back up and he reached his left arm along the top of the seat until his hand touched her far shoulder. He felt her shoulder stiffen and then relax as she moved closer and leaned toward· him. He slipped down lower in the seat so that her head could reach his shoulder and he felt the gentle touch of her brown hair on his neck above his shirt collar. He waited patiently and at last he could tell by her steady deep breathing that all fright had left her and all her thoughts were stilled.

The coach reached a rutted stretch and began to sway and the young man stirred and began to slide on the smooth leather of his seat. Sergeant Houck put up a foot and braced it against the seat edge and the young man's body rested against it. Sergeant Houck leaned his head back on the top of the seat. The stars came out in the clear sky and the running beat of the hoofs had the rhythm of a cavalry squad at a steady trot and gradually Sergeant Houck softened slightly into sleep.

Sergeant Houck awoke, as always, all at once and aware. The coach had stopped. From the sounds outside, fresh horses were being buckled into the traces. The first light of dawn was creeping into the coach. He raised his head and he realized that he was stiff.

The young man was awake. He was inspecting the vast leather sole of Sergeant Houck's shoe. His eyes flicked up and met Sergeant Houck's eyes and he grinned.

"That's impressive footwear," he whispered. "You'd need starch in the legs with hoofs like that." He sat up and stretched, long and reaching, like a lazy young animal. "Hell," he whispered again. "You must be stiff as a branding iron." He took hold of Sergeant Houck's leg at the knee and hoisted it slightly so that Sergeant Houck could bend it and ease the foot down to the floor without disturbing the sleeping woman leaning against him. He stretched out both hands and gently lifted the sleeping boy from Sergeant Houck's lap and sat back with the boy in his arms. The young man studied the boy's face. "Can't be yours," he whispered.

"No," whispered Sergeant Houck.

"Must have some Indian strain."

"Yes."

The young man whispered down at the sleeping boy. "You can't help that, can you, bub?"

"No," said Sergeant Houck suddenly, out loud. "He can't."

The woman jerked upright and pulled over to the window on her side, rubbing at her eyes. The boy woke up, wide awake on the instant and saw the unfamiliar face above him and began to squirm violently. The young man clamped his arms tighter. "Morning, ma'am,"

241

he said. "Looks like I ain't such a good nursemaid."

Sergeant Houck reached out a hand and picked up the boy by a grip on the small overalls and deposited him in a sitting position on the seat beside the young man. The boy sat very still.

The sun climbed into plain view and now the coach was stirring the dust of a well-worn road. It stopped where another road crossed and the young man inside pulled on his boots. He bobbed his head in the direction of a group of low buildings up the side road. "Think I'll try it there. They'll be peeling broncs about now and the foreman knows I can sit a saddle." He opened a door and jumped to the ground and turned to poke his head in. "Hope you make it right," he said. "Wherever you're heading." The door closed and he could be heard scrambling up the back of the coach to get his saddle. There was a thump as he and the saddle hit the ground and then voices began outside, rising in tone.

Sergeant Houck pushed his head through the window beside him. The young man and the driver were facing each other over the saddle. The young man was pulling the pockets of his Levis inside out. "Lookahere, Will," he said. "You know I'll kick in soon as I have some cash. Hell, I've hooked rides with you before."

"Not now no more," said the driver. "The company's sore. They hear of this they'd have my job. I'll have to hold the saddle."

"You touch that saddle and they'll pick you up in pieces from here to breakfast."

Sergeant Houck fumbled for his inside jacket pocket. He whistled. The two men turned. He looked hard at the young man. "There's something on the seat in here. Must have slipped out of your pocket."

The young man leaned in and saw the two silver dollars on the hard seat and looked up at Sergeant Houck. "You've been in spots yourself," he said.

"Yes," said Sergeant Houck.

The young man grinned. He picked up the two coins in one hand and swung the other to slap Sergeant Houck's leg, sharp and stinging and grateful. "Age ain't hurting you any, general," he said.

The coach started up and the woman looked at Sergeant Houck. The minutes passed and still she looked at him.

"If I'd had brains enough to get married," he said, "might be I'd have had a son. Might have been one like that."

The woman looked away, out her window. She reached up to pat at her hair and the firm line of her lips softened in the tiny imperceptible beginnings of a smile. The minutes passed and Sergeant Houck stirred again. "It's the upbringing that counts," he said and settled into silent immobility, watching the miles go by.

It was near noon when they stopped in Laramie and Sergeant Houck handed the woman out and tucked the boy under one arm and led the way to the waiting room. He settled the woman and the boy in two chairs and left them. He was back soon, driving a light buckboard wagon drawn by a pair of deep-barreled chestnuts. The wagon bed was well padded with layers of empty burlap bags. He went into the waiting room and picked up the boy and beckoned to the woman to follow. He put the boy down on the burlap bags and helped the woman up on the driving seat.

"Straight out the road, they tell me," he said. "About fifteen miles. Then right along the creek. Can't miss it."

He stood by the wagon, staring along the road. The woman leaned from the seat and clutched at his shoulder. Her voice was high and frightened. "You're going with me?" Her fingers clung to his service jacket. "Please! You've got to!"

Sergeant Houck put a hand over hers on his shoulder and released her fingers. "Yes. I'm going." He put the child in her lap and stepped to the seat and took the reins. The wagon moved forward.

"You're afraid," he said.

"They haven't told him," she said, "about the boy."

Sergeant Houck's hands tightened on the reins and the horses slowed to a walk. He clucked sharply to them and slapped the reins on their backs and they quickened again into a trot. The wagon topped a slight rise and the road sloped downward for a long stretch to where the green of trees and tall bushes showed in the distance. A jack rabbit started from the scrub growth by the roadside and leaped high and leveled out, a gray-brown streak. The horses shied and broke rhythm and quieted to a walk under the firm pressure of the reins. Sergeant Houck kept them at a walk, easing the heat out of their muscles, down the long slope to the trees. He let them step into the creek up to their knees and dip their muzzles in the clear running water. The front wheels of the wagon were in the creek and he reached behind him to find a tin dipper tucked among the burlap bags and leaned far out to dip up water for the woman and the boy and himself. He backed the team out of the creek and swung them into the wagon ruts leading along the bank to the right.

The creek was on their left and the sun was behind them, warm on their backs, and the shadows of the horses pushed ahead. The shadows were longer, stretching farther ahead, when they rounded a bend along the creek and the buildings came in sight, the two-room cabin and the several lean-to sheds and the rickety pole corral. A man was standing by one of the sheds and when Sergeant Houck stopped the team he came toward them and stopped about twenty feet away. He was not young, perhaps in his middle thirties, but with the young look of a man on whom the years have made no mark except that of the simple passing of time. He was tall, soft and loose-jointed in build, and indecisive in manner and movement. His eyes wavered as he looked at the woman, and the fingers of his hands hanging limp at his sides twitched as he waited for her to speak.

She climbed down her side of the wagon and faced him. She stood straight and the sun behind her shone on her hair. "Well, Fred," she said. "I'm here."

"Cora," he said. "It's been a long time, Cora. I didn't know you'd come so soon."

"Why didn't you come get me? Why didn't you, Fred?"

"I didn't rightly know what to do, Cora. It was all so mixed up. Thinking you were dead. Then hearing about you. And what happened. I had to think about things. And I couldn't get away easy. I was going to try maybe next week."

"I hoped you'd come. Right away when you heard."

His body twisted uneasily while his feet remained flat and motionless on the ground. "Your hair's still pretty," he said. "The way it used to be."

Something like a sob caught in her throat and she started toward him. Sergeant Houck stepped down on the other side of the wagon and walked off to the creek and kneeled to bend and wash the dust from his face. He stood drying his face with a handkerchief and watching the little eddies of the current around several stones in the creek. He heard the voices behind him.

"Wait, Fred. There's something you have to know."

"That kid? What's it doing here with you?"

"It's mine, Fred."

"Yours? Where'd you get it?"

"It's my child. Mine."

There was silence and then the man's voice, bewildered, hurt. "So it's really true what they said. About that Indian."

"Yes. He bought me. By their rules I belonged to him. I wouldn't be alive and here now, any other way. I didn't have any say about it."

There was silence again and then the man spoke, self-pity creeping into his tone. "I didn't count on anything like this."

Sergeant Houck walked back to the wagon. The woman seemed relieved at the interruption. "This is Sergeant Houck," she said. "He brought me all the way."

The man nodded his head and raised a hand to shove back the sandy hair that kept falling forward on his forehead. "I suppose I ought to thank you, soldier. All that trouble."

"No trouble," said Sergeant Houck.

The man pushed at the ground in front of him with one shoe, poking the toe into the dirt and studying it. "I suppose we ought to go inside. It's near suppertime. I guess you'll be taking a meal here, soldier, before you start back to town."

"Right," said Sergeant Houck. "And I'm tired. I'll stay the night, too. Start in the morning. Sleep in one of those sheds."

The man pushed at the ground more vigorously. The little pile of dirt in front of his shoe seemed to interest him a great deal. "All right, soldier. Sorry there's no quarters inside." He turned quickly and started for the cabin.

The woman took the boy from the wagon and followed him. Sergeant Houck unharnessed the horses and led them to the creek for a drink and to the corral and let them through the gate. He walked quietly to the cabin doorway and stopped just outside.

"For God's sake, Cora," the man was saying, "I don't see why you had to bring that kid with you. You could have told me about it. I didn't have to see him."

"What do you mean?"

"Why, now we've got the problem of how to get rid of him. Have to find a mission or some place that'll take him. Why didn't you leave him where he came from?"

"No! He's mine!"

"Good God, Cora! Are you crazy? Think you can foist off a thing like that on me?"

Sergeant Houck stepped through the doorway. "Thought I heard something about supper," he said. He looked around the small room, then let his eyes rest on the man. "I see the makings on those shelves. Come along, Mr. Sutliff. A woman doesn't want men cluttering about when she's getting a meal. Show me your place before it gets dark."

He stood, waiting, and the man scraped at the floor with one foot and slowly stood up and went with him.

They were well beyond earshot of the cabin when Sergeant Houck spoke again. "How long were you married? Before it happened?"

"Six years," said the man. "No, seven. It was seven when we lost the last place and headed this way with the train."

"Seven years," said Sergeant Houck. "And no child."

"It just didn't happen. I don't know why." The man stopped and looked sharply at Sergeant Houck. "Oh. So that's the way you're looking at it."

"Yes," said Sergeant Houck. "Now you've got one. A son."

"Not mine," said the man. "You can talk. It's not *your* wife. It's bad enough thinking of taking an Indian's leavings." He wiped his lips on his sleeve and spat in disgust. "I'll be damned if I'll take his kid."

"Not his any more. He's dead."

"Look, man. Look how it'd be. A damned little half-breed. Around all the time to make me remember what she did. A reminder of things I'd want to forget."

"Could be a reminder that she had some mightly hard going. And maybe come through the better for it."

"*She* had hard going! What about me? Thinking she was dead. Getting used to that. Maybe thinking of another woman. Then she comes back—and an Indian kid with her. What does that make me?"

"Could make you a man," said Sergeant Houck. "Think it over." He turned away and went to the corral and leaned on the rail, watching the horses roll the sweat-itches out of the dry sod. The man went slowly down by the creek and stood on the bank, pushing at the dirt with one shoe and kicking small pebbles into the water. The sun, holding to the horizon rim, dropped suddenly out of sight and dusk came swiftly to blur the outlines of the buildings. The woman appeared in the doorway and called and they went in. There was simple food on the table and the woman stood beside it. "I've already fed him," she said and moved her head toward the door to the inner room.

Sergeant Houck ate steadily and reached to refill his plate. The man picked briefly at the food before him and stopped, and the woman ate nothing at all. The man put his hands on the table edge and pushed back and stood up. He went to a side shelf and took a bottle and two thick cups and set them by his plate. He filled the cups a third full from the bottle and shoved one along the table boards toward Sergeant Houck. He lifted the other. His voice was bitter. "Happy home-coming," he said. He waited and Sergeant Houck took the other cup and they drank. The man lifted the bottle and poured himself another drink.

The woman looked quickly at him and away. "Please, Fred."

The man paid no attention. He reached with the bottle toward the other cup.

"No," said Sergeant Houck.

The man shrugged. "You can think better on whisky. Sharpens the mind." He set the bottle down and took his cup and drained it. Sergeant Houck fumbled in his right side pocket and found a short straight straw there and pulled it out and put one end in his mouth and chewed slowly on it. The man and the woman sat still, opposite each other at the table, and seemed to forget his quiet presence. They stared everywhere except at each other. Yet their attention was plainly concentrated on each other. The man spoke first. His voice was restrained, carrying conscious patience.

"Look, Cora. You wouldn't want to do that to me. You can't mean what you said before."

Her voice was determined. "He's mine."

"Now, Cora. You don't want to push it too far. A man can take just so much. I didn't know what to do after I heard about you. But I was all ready to forgive you. And now you—"

"Forgive me!" She knocked against her chair rising to her feet. Hurt and bewilderment made her voice ragged as she repeated the words. "Forgive me?" She turned and ran into the inner room. The handleless door banged shut behind her.

The man stared after her and shook his head and reached again for the bottle.

"Enough's enough," said Sergeant Houck.

The man shrugged in quick irritation, "For you maybe," he said and poured himself another drink. "Is there any reason you should be noseying in on this?"

"My orders," said Sergeant Houck, "were to deliver them safely. Both of them."

"You've done that." said the man. He lifted the cup and drained it and set it down carefully. "They're here."

"Yes," said Sergeant Houck. "They're here." He stood up and stepped to the outside door and looked into the night. He waited a moment until his eyes were accustomed to the darkness and could distinguish objects faintly in the starlight. He stepped out and went to the pile of straw behind one of the sheds and took an armload and carried it back by the cabin and dropped it at the foot of a tree by one corner. He sat on it, his legs stretched out, his shoulders against the tree, and broke off a straw stem and chewed slowly on it. After a while his jaws stopped their slow slight movement and his head sank forward and his eyes closed.

Sergeant Houck woke up abruptly. He was on his feet in a moment, and listening. He heard the faint sound of voices in the cabin, indistinct but rising as the tension rose in them. He went toward the doorway and stopped just short of the rectangle of light from the lamp.

"You're not going to have anything to do with me!" The woman's voice was harsh with stubborn anger. "Not until this has been settled right!"

"Aw, come on, Cora." The man's voice was fuzzy, slow-paced. "We'll talk about that in the morning."

"No!"

"All right!" Sudden fury made the man's voice shake. "You want it settled now! Well, it's settled! We're getting rid of that damn' kid first thing tomorrow!"

"No!"

"What gave you the idea you've got any say around here after what you did? I'm the one to say what's to be done. You don't be careful, maybe I won't take you back."

"Maybe I don't want you to!"

"So damn' finicky all of a sudden! After being with that Indian and maybe a lot more!"

Sergeant Houck stepped through the doorway. The man's back was to him, and he spun him around and his right hand smacked against the side of the man's face and sent him staggering against the wall.

"Forgetting your manners won't help," said Sergeant Houck. He looked around, and the woman had disappeared into the inner room. The man leaned against the wall, rubbing his cheek, and she came out, the boy in her arms, and ran toward the outer door.

"Cora!" the man shouted. "Cora!"

She stopped, a brief hesitation in flight. "I don't belong

to you," she said and was gone through the doorway. The man pushed out from the wall and started after her and the great bulk of Sergeant Houck blocked the way.

"You heard her," said Sergeant Houck. "She doesn't belong to anybody now. Nobody but that boy."

The man stared at him and some of the fury went out of his eyes and he stumbled to his chair at the table and reached for the bottle. Sergeant Houck watched him a moment, then turned and quietly went outside. He walked toward the corral and as he passed the second shed, she came out of the darker shadows and her voice, low and intense, whispered at him.

"I've got to go. I can't stay here."

Sergeant Houck nodded and went on to the corral. He harnessed the horses quickly and with a minimum of sound. He finished buckling the traces and stood straight and looked toward the cabin. He walked to the doorway and stepped inside. The man was leaning forward in his chair, his elbows on the table, staring at the empty bottle.

"It's finished," said Sergeant Houck. "She's leaving now."

The man shook his head and pushed at the bottle with one forefinger. "She can't do that." He looked up at Sergeant Houck and sudden rage began to show in his eyes. "She can't do that! She's my wife!"

"Not any more," said Sergeant Houck. "Best forget she ever came back." He started toward the door and heard the sharp sound of the chair scraping on the floor behind him. The man's voice rose, shrilling up almost into a shriek.

"Stop!" The man rushed to the wall rack and grabbed the rifle there and held it low and aimed it at Sergeant Houck. "Stop!" He was breathing deeply and he fought for control of his voice. "You're not going to take her away!"

Sergeant Houck turned slowly. He stood still, a motionless granite shape in the lamplight.

"Threatening an Army man," said Sergeant Houck. "And with an empty gun."

The man wavered and his eyes flicked down at the rifle. In the second of indecision Sergeant Houck plunged toward him and one huge hand grasped the gun barrel and pushed it aside and the shot thudded harmlessly into the cabin wall. He wrenched the gun from the man's grasp and his other hand took the man by the shirt front and pushed him down into the chair.

"No more of that," said Sergeant Houck. "Best sit quiet." He looked around the room and found the box of cartridges on a shelf and he took this with the rifle and went to the door. "Look around in the morning and you'll find these." He went outside and tossed the gun up on the roof of one of the sheds and dropped the little box by the pile of straw and kicked some straw over it. He went to the wagon and stood by it and the woman came out of the darkness, carrying the boy.

The wagon wheels rolled silently. The small creakings of the wagon body and the thudding rhythm of the horses' hoofs were distinct, isolated sounds in the night. The creek was on their right and they followed the road back the way they had come. The woman moved on the seat, shifting the boy's weight from one arm to the other, until Sergeant Houck took him by the overalls and lifted him and reached behind to lay him on the burlap bags. "A good boy," he said. "Has the Indian way of taking things without yapping. A good way."

The thin new tracks in the dust unwound endlessly under the wheels and the waning moon climbed through the scattered bushes and trees along the creek.

"I have relatives in Missouri," said the woman. "I could go there."

Sergeant Houck fumbled in his side pocket and found a straw and put this in his mouth and chewed slowly on it. "Is that what you want?"

"No."

They came to the main-road crossing and swung left and the dust thickened under the horses' hoofs. The lean dark shape of a coyote slipped from the brush on one side and bounded along the road and disappeared on the other side.

"I'm forty-seven," said Sergeant Houck. "Nearly thirty of that in the Army. Makes a man rough."

The woman looked straight ahead and a small smile showed in the corners of her mouth.

"Four months," said Sergeant Houck, "and this last hitch's done. I'm thinking of homesteading on out in the Territory." He chewed on the straw and took it between a thumb and forefinger and flipped it away. "You could get a room at the settlement."

"I could," said the woman. The horses slowed to a

walk, breathing deeply, and he let them hold the steady, plodding pace. Far off a coyote howled and others caught the signal and the sounds echoed back and forth in the distance and died away into the night silence.

"Four months," said Sergeant Houck. "That's not so long."

"No," said the woman. "Not too long."

A breeze stirred across the brush and she put out a hand and touched his shoulder. Her fingers moved down along his upper arm and curved over the big muscles there and the warmth of them sank through the cloth of his worn service jacket. She dropped her hand in her lap again and looked ahead along the ribbon of the road. He clucked to the horses and urged them again into a trot and the small creakings of the wagon body and the dulled rhythm of the hoofs were gentle sounds in the night.

The late moon climbed and its pale light shone slantwise down on the moving wagon, on the sleeping boy and the woman looking straight ahead, and on the great solid figure of Sergeant Houck.

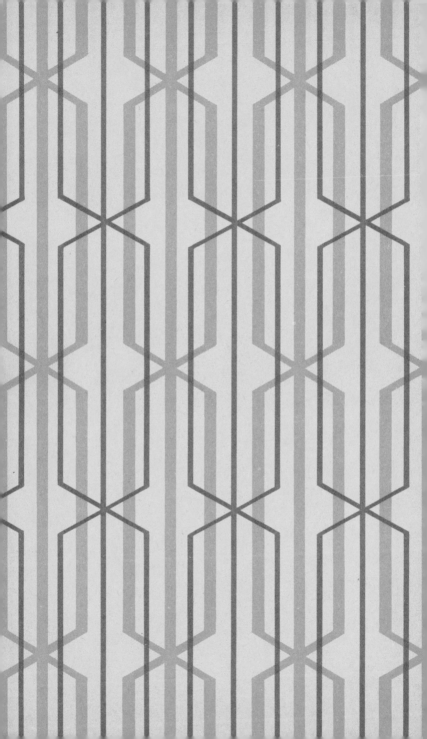